"[Gillian is] A nev

~Wayne Thomas Batson, Author of The Door Within series, the Dark Sea Annals, and the Dreamtreader books~

"Rarely do I find an allegory that grips me as powerfully as a fantasy story, but *Out Of Darkness Rising* did just that. Gillian Bronte Adams has crafted a wonderful story that will remind you of the potency of Christ's sacrifice for our sins. A truly great allegory that I am pleased to recommend to lovers of fantasy fiction."

~Scott Appleton, Author of The Sword of the Dragon series and the Neverqueen series~

"Beware of Gillian Bronte Adams! Her writing will catch you by the scruff of your tunic and drag you into one marvelous adventure after another. Of course ... if that is what you want, then by all means pick up her latest novella, *Out Of Darkness Rising* — you won't be disappointed!"

~Robert Treskillard, Award Winning Author of the Merlin Spiral~

"There's a reason authors don't often write allegory. It is easy to do poorly, but fiendishly tricky to do well. Gillian Bronte Adams shows us what allegory looks like when it is done well. She has given us a gift in the form of this book, with crisp prose and compelling characters. Ms. Adams is a writer to watch."

~A. T. Ross, Author of The Word and the Sword series~

Out of Darkness Rising

An Allegory of Redemption

Gillian Bronte Adams

Magpie Eclectic Press

Dedication:

To all who are weary and heavy laden,

this book is for you.

To Anna
Hope you enjoy!
Jillian Bronte Adams
Isaiah 9:2

PART ONE

Darkness

Betrayal.

The word had a pleasant ring to it. Arientyl could become accustomed to the shape of it on his tongue, the ring of it in his ears, the tint of it covering his clothes and staining the skin of his sword-hand. After centuries of bowing and scraping and smiling through gritted teeth, the freedom that came with finally allowing the mask to fall was pure relief.

Who could have imagined betrayal could be so sweet?

The wet thud of his boots echoed before him down the stone hallway toward the massive hardwood door that led to the King's chambers. *So close now... so close.* His hand involuntarily tightened about the grip of his sword. He allowed himself a quickening of breath as he envisioned driving the blade into the King's heart and feeling the strong form that had ever stood in his way finally crumble, the breath of opposition finally release in vain.

He halted before the door and lifted his hand to the latch.

A whisper of movement behind sent him spinning into a defensive position. The figure of a warrior stood in the center of the hallway, surrounded by the bodies of the slain, cloak hem soaking up the blood that was Arientyl's handiwork.

There was no mistaking that sword stance.

Or the one it belonged to, the King's own son.

Arientyl swung away from the door, regaining room to maneuver. Pinning himself down early on would be a good way to consign his corpse to a watery grave in the Loch that bordered the Kingdom. One on one, control of the field of battle was just as important as skill.

Without a word, the Prince undid the clasp of his cloak with one hand and allowed the billowing blue length to drop into the blood at his feet.

For a moment, they stood thus in silence, until the weight of his opponent's unwavering gaze pressured Arientyl to speak. "Twenty seven." He advanced a step, muscles tight, anticipating the attack. "I thought you might care to know the record of the slain. The number of deaths required to draw you into battle. Seven knights and twenty of your precious peasants are wallowing in their own blood, all because you and your father refused to acknowledge me."

In the stillness, the echoes of his voice ricocheted down the hallway, like mocking laughter rising from the slain. But the Prince simply stepped to one side and lowered his blade.

Arientyl tightened his grip on his sword until his hand shook. He required no prattling magician to divine the warrior's intent in opening a way of escape through the slaughter. Even now, it seemed to say, a path of return remained.

But that path required bended knee and a life of subservience.

The Prince's arrogance surpassed all bounds. Was he truly vain enough to suppose that a meaningless gesture would be enough to divert Arientyl from his purpose?

Disgust stoked his tongue to action. "You need not feign surprise. You knew this day was coming—you *must* have known." He spat on the flagstones between them. "It is past time I take my stand. I defy you and your father. I will not yield. Defeat me if you can."

The Prince approached, his steps weighted and pulsing with purpose. "I can."

Arientyl did not wait for his foe's sword to rise but launched straight into the attack—quick, forceful strokes meant to end the battle before it truly began. Months of careful planning, all the time knowing that this most dangerous confrontation was inevitable, had offered no other solution.

He must win quickly or not at all.

But his flurry of blows failed to beat past his opponent's guard, each stroke blocked with equal force and unyielding strength. So he pulled back ever so slightly, watching for an opening, then lunged at the Prince's side.

His boots slipped on the blood-slick floor. He slammed into the wall and spun out of reach to regain his balance, but the Prince had already drawn back, ostensibly yielding him time to regain his stance. *Ever the gentleman.* Sickening, that's what it was, this incessant display of impossible honor.

Honor was dead.

And the Prince would learn it ere the night was done.

Over his challenger's shoulder, he caught a glimpse of the hardwood door, and understanding sank like a stone in his stomach. Caught up in the scuffle, he had allowed himself to be drawn away from his objective. Now the Prince stood between him and the King's chambers, placing him in the position of the attacker and his opponent on the defensive.

In the dozens of scenarios he had envisioned, not one had succeeded once the King's son gained the strategic position before the doors.

He needed to regain the advantage. Force—no, *trick* the Prince into the offensive. A calculated risk.

He lunged with the next thrust, allowed his blade to be turned aside with careless ease, and stumbled as if about to lose his balance. The action bared his side for just a hair's breadth of a moment to his foe's blade. If he struck—and he must—Arientyl was quick enough to turn aside the weapon and use the momentum to push past and recover his post before the doors.

But the strike didn't come.

Braced for the impact, he twisted to block from high guard, only to slice through thin air and stagger to regain his balance. Through the gap beneath his upraised arms, he caught sight of the determined set of the Prince's jaw and the anger in his eyes, and for the first time since embarking on this night of betrayal, a tremor of fear wormed through his stomach.

Guided by instinct over sight, he felt the coming stroke rather than saw it and shifted to parry. The blow crashed against his blade, followed by a barrage of relentless strikes that drove him back. His boots skidded for purchase on the slick stone. He stumbled over the body of one of the peasant guards who had tried to halt his attack.

And still the blows came.

At last, the Prince was on the offensive. His ruse had worked. The battle now would be a matter of endurance and cunning—no longer the quick affair he had desired—but if there was one area where Arientyl knew himself unmatched, it was in the matter of scheming.

So why did he feel that the mastery of this battle lay in his enemy's hands?

*****

Dust and ashes clogged his throat. Gasping for breath, Arientyl rolled out of the rubbish heap and staggered across the cluttered yard behind the castle kitchen, away from the blade seeking his blood. He limped with extravagant flair as he skirted the stacks of barrels and crates that transformed the yard into a maze.

Weak—that is what he must appear—defeated.

Such a tactic alone could aid him now that the element of surprise had been lost. Let the Prince underestimate him, as the King had—as everyone always did. It would only make it easier for him to conquer in the end.

The thought lent speed to his retreat—out the gates of the castle, ducking through the orchard, dashing along the furrows of newly ploughed fields, and headlong down the rocky hillside, pausing to fight only when his enemy's footsteps too closely echoed his own. He guarded with wild, frantic strokes—not panicked enough to cause the Prince to doubt, but just desperate enough to convince him of victory—until a cool breath of wind stirred the hair plastered to his skull and whispered that the Loch was near.

Casting aside all deception, Arientyl resumed the firm stance of a warrior and blocked the next stroke, sliding forward and catching his enemy's blade against his crossguard. He grinned, ignoring his quivering arms and legs. Through the locked swords, he caught a glimpse of his adversary's sweat-stained face and gritted teeth.

"You honestly thought it would be so easy to defeat me, didn't you?"

No response.

He should have expected as much. Such haughty disdain was typical of the King's son. More than a weak taunt was required to provoke the Prince's wrath.

Knowing that did little to cool Arientyl's wrath.

The rocks slipped under his left boot, and he lurched to the side to keep from falling. His sword broke free, and he circled beyond the reach of the Prince's blade, grateful for a moment to catch his breath.

"They are not like us, you know. Your precious peasants. They are but a breath—a leaf that withers in autumn's wake and is blown away. But we... *we* are enduring. Twenty of them along with seven of your knights had no hope against me. I watched them fall just as a leaf at the first breath of winter—watched the life bleed from their wounds—and through the pain in their eyes, I saw understanding."

He lunged, a feint to the left, followed by a slash at the midsection. Both swords met with a jarring crash, and he forced the Prince back a pace.

"In the end," he snarled between blows, "they met death face to face and knew me for what I am—a force to be reckoned with. But you... and your father... are incapable of admitting it!"

Caution warned him to focus, to chain his tongue until his rival lay expiring at his feet, to arrange the web of moves and countermoves that would gain him victory. But his blood called for attack. His strokes fell faster and faster, and his feet beat a clattering tattoo over the rocks as he pressed the Prince toward the beach.

Then his heels sank into white sand. Over his enemy's shoulder, he caught a glimpse of deep blue: the Loch—a fitting place for the final battle. Submerged in the Loch, his foe would pass out of sight and memory forever.

Drunk with the promise of victory, Arientyl threw all his force into the next stroke. The blow beat past the Prince's guard and glanced off his mailed shoulder. Before he could follow up with a second stroke, his rival once again stepped back and lowered his sword.

Arientyl paused, muscles gathered for the next attack, hesitant to strike until he discovered the purpose of this new ploy. It was too soon for a surrender, and the King's son would never yield so easily.

Was this another pitiful endeavor to tempt him to repentance?

"My father trained you well." Sword gripped in both hands, the Prince brought it into a middle guard position, point angling up level with his eyes. "You were a great warrior—his finest—but in betraying him, you have lost more than you can imagine."

White flames burst from the sword and wreathed the blade.

Arientyl stumbled back a step, blinking. The Prince lunged at him, and he brought his sword up just in time to deflect the blade from his heart. He spun to the right, but his foe was already there, waiting for him.

He dropped under a slash, rolled, and rose, sword guarding his head from a downward strike. Sparks flew when the weapons clashed. The heat seared his face and hands. Sand, stirred by the rapid pace of their feet, hung in the air and set his eyes watering. He struggled to calm his ragged breathing and squelch the rising tide of uncertainty in his chest, blocking and guarding mechanically as his muscles obeying instincts his emotions would not.

Water swelled around his feet, slowing his retreat.

He—not the Prince—had been forced into the Loch.

A dull ache settled in his sword arm. Surely after such a fight the King's son felt the strain as well. Arientyl searched his opponent's face for signs of weariness as the Prince drew back for another strike... a final strike. Determination steeled his face and his eyes reflected the white fire of his sword, but a tear slipped down his cheek.

Arientyl faltered and his grip loosened.

The stroke descended and the clash rang in his ears. He stared at his empty, tingling hand and at the sword flying up the beach to clatter against the rocks. His legs bent without his command, and he stumbled to his knees in the water, in a supplicating position. His heart burned with anger at the thought, but he could not rise. The flaming sword lowered to rest against his throat.

"You chose darkness over light," the Prince declared.

Arientyl forced his gaze past the blinding light of the sword to his enemy's hand tightening on the hilt—knuckles white, muscles tense to deliver the killing blow. He drew one final breath and held it, marveling at the pervasive tang of blood that soiled his clothing and seeped into the air.

The Prince relaxed and withdrew his sword. "Your end has not yet come." The tear shimmered like molten gold on his cheek.

Arientyl's lungs filled with air once more and his shoulders sagged with relief, only to snap back to rigidity, cursing his moment of weakness. He had come seeking victory or death. He would not accept mercy, nor would a true warrior grant it, not after walking through the bodies strewn along the flagstones of the corridor.

Always, the King's son had been weak.

"Do you now regret denying my claim? You should." He spat at the Prince's boots. "You know the law—blood must pay the price of wrongdoing. The deaths of your precious peasants rest on your head and that of your father. Mayhap it was my hand that spilled their blood, but the fault resides with you and you alone. And you *cannot* defeat me, and I will *never* yield—not until I gain my rightful place. Though the mountains crumble into the sea, I will never cease fighting you." His hand plunged to the sheath in his boot, and he staggered upright, dagger flashing.

Light blazed from the Prince's sword and collected around him. The flood of malice dried on Arientyl's tongue. His limbs stiffened until he could not move.

The Prince's voice shook the shore like thunder. "Go to the darkness, creature of evil, for darkness you have become."

Brilliant white light rushed toward Arientyl. The dagger sizzled in his grasp like a red-hot coal, and his hand flew open, releasing the blade. He closed his eyes and clasped his face in his hands, but it was useless. Light surrounded him, searing his eyes beneath the lids, boring into his mind until he could sense nothing but scorching whiteness.

The light slowly eased.

Wind roared in his ears, and he realized he was flying backwards, flung into the air by an incredible force. Grasping blindly for something to break his fall, he screamed his fury to the skies.

Then everything was gone.

Blackness.

Nothing but blackness all around. Smothering, cold, inescapable darkness, over and under, everywhere he turned. A choked cry rose in his throat. He thrashed, limbs flailing in search of something—*anything*. But the darkness no longer surrounded him; it had become a part of him.

He was the darkness.

Strangely, the thought brought a sliver of comfort. Darkness meant concealment, a cloak for the schemer, a shield from the intensity of the light and his own shame at defeat.

Arientyl stretched forth a hand to explore his surroundings. It felt weightless, but a strange resistance tugged at his fingers as he moved them back and forth.

Cold... wet...

He was floating underwater.

Like a fire gnawing at his bones, panic flared in his chest. He struggled to find the surface, straining to see through the pitch black, but he could no longer tell up from down. Despair froze his arms. He hugged them to his chest and allowed himself to sink.

Down, down.

Seconds stretched on like the eternity he had spent bowed before the King's throne, yielding to the Prince, protecting the peasants, biding his time to claim the glory that should have been his from the start. Recollection flooded his mouth with the bitter tang of ash. He tore away from the memory, back to the present where the seconds had become minutes, and the minutes seemed thousands of years. Surely he should be dead by now. At the very least, his lungs should have been screaming for air, his limbs seized with a last desperate attempt to survive, his consciousness fading to dull nothingness…

Or perhaps this *was* death.

Arientyl pressed a hand to his face, but instead of soft flesh, hard, scaly skin met his touch. Slime covered the scales and clung to his hand as he jerked it away.

No amount of self-control could contain his fear now.

What was happening to him?

He forced himself to move, no longer caring that every yard traveled might bring him deeper below the Loch's surface. Fish-like, he wove through the cold water, muscles strained to the utmost, propelling him at an increasing speed.

What have I become?

Faster and faster he went, rushing through the black depths, until it seemed that he must be fairly flying. A faint glimmer appeared ahead, a ripple of distorted light in the darkness. He sped toward it and burst out of the water into gray morning. Water shot into the air around him and cascaded down with a mighty roar. A moment later, he plunged back into the dark. Cold swallowed him, but he kept his bearing this time and pushed his way up again to thrust his head and shoulders out into open air.

Water swam in his eyes, and he blinked, squinting against the glare of the half-light that stabbed deep within his head. He turned a slow circle. Endless stretches of water surrounded him on all sides, vast and unbroken by land until they faded from sight on the horizon in a misty cloud of gray and blue.

The Loch.

So this it to be my prison.

Down into the water he gazed, and slowly raised his hands until they broke the surface. A cry tore from his throat; he did not try to suppress it. Instead of hands, two hideous scaled claws met his gaze—warped and disfigured, with webbed fingers and curved talons. He held both claws to his eyes, transfixed.

How did this happen?

Desperate for his reflection, he peered into the Loch. Water droplets fell from his jaw, spreading ripples that disturbed the smooth mirror he sought. He shook his head, sending wet spray flying, then waited.

When the Loch became still at last, a monstrous face stared back at him. Slanted, red-rimmed eyes sat above a long, bony snout which housed a gaping mouth filled with jagged fangs. Black smoke poured from his nostrils, settling over the Loch like a cloud, and flames flickered in the back of his mouth.

Heart thundering in his chest, Arientyl tore himself away from his reflection and looked back over his shoulder to behold the rest of his body. It wound across the waves, a sinuous, snake-like form, coated in black scales.

Flames burst from his throat and stabbed the water.

The Prince.

Cloud steamed above him, dark and broiling like the blackness within his heart. Arientyl dove, his powerful arms and log-like tail providing speed and momentum as he shot through the deep.

I will never cease fighting you.

His own words rang in his mind, and he screamed them into the darkness. "I will never cease fighting you!"

*****

Arientyl cursed inwardly at the morning light and raised a claw to shield his face from the dazzling brilliance of the sun. His ears rang with the laughter and singing echoing from the distant shore where he, robed in the blood of the slain, had battled the King's son and been defeated only the day before.

Or had it been centuries? There was no measurement of time in the depths of the Loch, no way to count the hours or years he had been brooding beneath the foundations of the earth.

Regardless, the sight that met his eyes was a far cry from that of the battle, of dust and flames and bloodstained footprints. The grassy hillside fell to meet the Loch in a succession of rolling dunes and heather-crowned hillocks. On the hilltop, a line of trees swayed in the breeze, shading a tilled field. Peasants moved across the landscape, appearing as little more than specks of color amidst the brilliant green, like wildflowers in a remote meadow. They bustled about in a whirlwind of activity; some worked in the field, others fished from the shore, and still others moved through the trees gathering the fruit harvest.

Arientyl clenched his jaw. To his ears, their laughing voices sounded harsh and empty, like the clatter of clanging bells. That's what peasants were, after all—brass bells crafted for the purpose of pealing the King's praises, while the King and the Prince manipulated the ropes.

On the shoreline, two figures walked side by side, the murmur of their voices drifting across the water. The younger stopped and threw his head back to laugh. The sound stoked Arientyl's rage, and fire flared from his mouth with a rush of black smoke.

It was his enemy the King… and that cursed Prince.

He turned to leave, but one of the peasants caught his eye on the opposite end of the beach: a young girl stooped in the shallows of the Loch, splashing in the water. Sinking so that only his eyes were not submerged, Arientyl drifted toward the shore. Something about her expression captured his gaze—a look of boundless wonder and curiosity and the capacity for so much more. Dark hair slipped over her face as she played, and Arientyl unconsciously lifted a claw to brush it aside, as if the distance that separated them was a matter of inches rather than yards.

"Hadriel!"

Arientyl jerked back at the Prince's merry voice and could not keep a snarl from rising in his throat. The child stood and held her arms out. Breaking off his conversation with his father, the King's son ran over to her and swept her up, swinging her around his head and setting her down in the sand. She shrieked with joyful laughter and he joined in. He dropped beside her and watched as she started building a sandcastle.

But her hands were too small for the task, and the sand crumbled beneath her unskilled fingers. At last she raised imploring eyes. Chuckling, the Prince knelt and set to work. With his large, strong hands aiding her little ones, the sandcastle soon rose from the ground and towered over her head. She flung a handful of sand in the air and danced around her castle, giggling, until the Prince caught her up, set her on his shoulders, and ran back across the beach to his father.

He loves her. He truly loves these weak, pathetic, time-bound villagers.

The thought struck a chord in Arientyl's heart. Despite its ultimate failure, his painfully orchestrated attack had begun on the right course, even if he had not realized its full potential at the time. The peasants were both his enemy's weakness and his best weapon. Slaying twenty of the peasant guards and seven knights had been a hefty blow, but it was not enough... not nearly enough to sate the rage that burned within his chest.

He was almost grateful the attack had failed. Merely slaying the King would not suffice, not when he could see him suffer first. It would be infinitely more rewarding to behold the King's sorrow when his beloved peasants forsook him for another.

His vow to fight repeated in his mind as his thoughts materialized out of the mist and formulated into a plan. Arientyl cast one last glance toward the joyous villagers on shore. His gaze lingered a moment over the Prince and the child now dancing on the beach, then with a hiss, he dove into the water, returning to the deep and welcomed darkness.

*****

Fifteen years later

A crack of thunder broke the peace of the autumn afternoon. Hadriel paused, apple in hand, halfway between the tree and her basket, and peered up through the rows of arching branches at the approaching storm clouds. The crisp air burned her lungs, but she took a deep breath anyway, savoring the smell of coming rain wafting through the orchard.

Roald, the King's chief harvester, appeared at her side, grizzled head cocked to keep a weather eye on the sky. "Storm's coming," he stated. "Bring what you've gathered and we'll pack it away. We'd best get indoors before it hits."

All around her, the villagers on gathering duty hastened to obey, collecting baskets and ladders, and hurrying to the storehouses. But Hadriel hesitated. The storms that swept off the Loch held no terror for her. The rising winds seemed to call her name, sending a thrill racing through her veins, summoning her to the edge of the world—the edge of her world—where he would be waiting.

She glanced over her shoulder, but the rest of the villagers were hastening to cover. There was no one watching.

Discarding her basket, she raced from the orchard, across the field, and down the hill to the beach. Her hair streamed back from her face as she ran, sand flying beneath her feet. She flung out her arms, exulting in freedom.

Breathless, she halted at the edge of the Loch. Thrashing water surged to beat the shore and tugged at her feet as it retreated. She shivered as the cold liquid swirled around her ankles, soaking the hem of her skirt.

Storm clouds sped toward her. Dark water faded into dark sky. Seeking the horizon, Hadriel strained to break the limitations of distance and sight. Who knew what lands lay beyond the Loch? What wonders might she behold if she were not bound to the shore?

"I know," a familiar voice said beside her. Deep and yet soft, it sounded both warm and friendly, like the honey she gathered from the King's beehives on summer afternoons. It made her feel older and wiser than her scant eighteen years. "There are countless lands out there, Hadriel. Wondrous and fair beyond all you can imagine."

"But unlike you, *I* cannot see them." Hadriel turned to the speaker. His ability to move soundlessly through the water continually astounded her. But he was never far away on days like this when she wandered down to the Loch, dreaming of distant marvels.

The Serpent's neck and forearms rested on the shore while the rest of his body stretched out gracefully across the Loch. His shining black scales glinted midnight blue in the glare of the approaching storm. "You could always come with me," he purred.

Her spine tingled. "You know I can't."

"Of course... the King's command. I had nearly forgotten. What a pity," he sighed. "The Loch has always fascinated you. I *know*. You are drawn to the mystery of what lies beyond its waters."

"But only from a distance."

"Why not admit the truth?" The Serpent's voice was a tender whisper near her ear. "You long to cross it, and why shouldn't you? What is the harm?"

She pulled away. "Because the King himself set the boundaries, and I trust him. What more need be said? We are not allowed across the Loch, and that is the end of the matter."

The great head shook slowly. "Surely not! It seems such an odd command. So stifling, so pointless and arbitrary.

Have you never wondered what is truly out there that the King doesn't want you to see?"

Her throat tightened. "I'm not a fool. I know there must be *some* reason, but I don't know what it is, and you won't tell me. You hint and you whisper, but I want answers, not more questions." She spun away and dropped into the sand, arms crossed over her chest.

The Serpent's head stooped, and she could almost see the debate flashing in his eyes. "Yes," he said at last. "You are ready." With a rustle of scales, he leaned in, and Hadriel scooted closer to hear the scarcely whispered words. "In the middle of the Loch is an island…"

His voice drifted into tantalizing silence in which the heavy puffs of his hot breath seemed louder than the distant thunder. Hadriel held her tongue, waiting for him to speak, until she could contain her curiosity no longer.

"An island?"

"Full of green growing things." The words dripped from his tongue like liquid gold. "An island of life and endless knowledge… where wonders abound and questions are never without answers… an island where each man is his own king."

King.

Hadriel cast an anxious glance over her shoulder toward the lofty towers of the palace crowning the green hill, and her stomach twisted. What if the King was watching? But she had done nothing wrong. Searching for answers was not forbidden.

"You wonder why I have never answered you before. It is because you were not yet ready to accept the fact that much of what you believe is, in fact, a lie. The Island is the paradise of your dreams, kept secret by your arrogant, selfish King. He has hidden it from you, his obedient subjects, so that he alone can possess its wonders."

In the face of such a dangerous accusation, Hadriel found it impossible to sit still. She shot to her feet and retreated to a safe distance several paces away. "How could *you* know this?"

The Serpent sighed. "I was not always as I am now. Once I was the King's chief knight, most trusted in counsel and privy to all his confidences. Driven by his own vainglory, he took me to the Island to boast of its riches, and as we stood on the deck of his ship, he pledged me to secrecy, never imagining that I would find fault with his greed. You may have heard my name—though any stories you would have been told are doubtless lies. Arientyl I once was, and I served the King faithfully for centuries beyond count."

"Arientyl." Hadriel wrapped her tongue around the unfamiliar title. "I don't know that name."

The Serpent hissed and black smoke drifted from his mouth. "*This* is what I received for my service. Bound in the form of a serpent, imprisoned in this Loch for daring to speak against the King's pride. I am nothing now... even less than nothing; my own name is buried in the ashes of the past. But I cannot remain silent while your people dwell in ignorance of the wonders that lie within reach, oblivious to the King's duplicity."

A chill blast of wind struck the shore, whipping strands of her dark hair across her face. Hadriel's teeth chattered, and she hugged her arms to her chest, trying to reconcile the image of the King she carried in her mind with the tyrant the Serpent's words painted. Ever the King appeared wise and kind—stern, yes, but not cruel or treacherous. A glimpse of smiling blue eyes danced across her vision, accompanied by the distant echo of joyful laughter—her laughter. Surely the Prince, at least, was innocent of any blame. Perhaps he too had been deceived, like the peasants.

"You say you trust the King." The Serpent's voice hummed beside her ear, and she stumbled back to maintain her distance. "But tell me truthfully, have you never *once* doubted the validity of his commands? What cause do you honestly have to trust him? You are one of his many slaves—he has every reason to placate you into unthinking submission. But I am unbiased. What have I to gain from misleading you?"

His words carried the force of reason, and all the excuses she could dream up bent before it. To forbid the villagers access to the wonders across the Loch reeked of hidden purpose. What other motive could the King possess but to reserve the best for himself? She shook her head, and a tear slipped down one cheek, though whether it was summoned by the wind or her own sorrowful thoughts she could not say.

The Serpent's eyes widened and a hiss of sympathy emanated from his gaping mouth. "You are hurt; that is understandable. It wounds you to discover the truth. You are all too trusting, as I once was." His voice fell into the deep purr of a great cat.

Hadriel tore her gaze away. The wind now whipped the Loch into a boiling brew of tossing waves, churning like the ache pounding in her chest. Before her lay freedom in all its wild fury. The castle on the hill behind seemed nothing more than a cage—stolid and unbending, like the commands of the King.

"You and I are not so different, Hadriel. You are bound by the King's command, as I was… chained to his service. And yet you chafe at the confines of serfdom." Scorching breaths puffed across her ear. "Courage is yours to throw aside the yoke and reason for yourself. You need not remain in senseless obedience to such a King."

Hadriel looked into the Serpent's face. Sorrow etched his brow, and a tear glimmered in the creases beneath his right eye. His eyes drew her gaze—deeper than the untold depths of the Loch, luminous with an internal fire, fueled not by sorrow but by rage.

She shrank back, but the Serpent spoke again, his voice quelling her impulse to flee.

"The King betrayed you and abused your trust and love. Why follow him still? Come with me to the Island, where you can be like the King, knowing all things, having all things, and ruling all things." His voice again faded to a whisper. "Come…"

Reflected in his eyes, Hadriel beheld a hazy vision of a fair green island crowned with luscious plants beneath a crystalline sky. It beckoned to her across the waves, and something within her stirred until every part of her being yearned to set foot upon that verdant shore.

"Come," the Serpent repeated as he slipped further into the water.

Hadriel licked her dry lips. Her breath rasped in her throat, and she clenched her hands to stop shaking. She took a step forward, then another.

The cold water met her shins.

She recoiled and fled to the safety of the shore. Her head spun, and she gripped it in both hands, gasping for breath.

"What is wrong, little one?"

"I can't go. I can't." She took a deep breath, striving to regain her composure. "Not alone."

The Serpent smiled, and it was the wide-stretched grin of a fox. "Do you think you are the only free heart among the peasants? That you alone have the eyes to see through the King's deceit and the courage to act? There are others waiting to join us even now. Come and see."

He slithered into the Loch, and she followed along the shore, hastening to keep pace with his powerful strokes.

Around the next curve, the beach vanished at the base of a steep slope. She scaled the slope, one eye turned to the Serpent in the water below, until she reached the top of a rocky headland overlooking a sheltered bay. The Serpent reared up in the water and clutched the side of the cliff with his claws, his chin resting on the edge near her feet.

"Behold," he declared, "the enlightened few!"

Nearly thirty peasants stood on the shingled beach that bordered the bay. Men, women, and children clutched bundles to their chests and peered eagerly at the Loch, waiting.

People like her. *Free hearts,* the Serpent called them.

The sound of it entranced her.

"You are not alone, Hadriel. There are twenty seven of them below. They too have come to realize that the King rules through a façade of kindness to conceal his own hidden purpose. But the best deception can only remain strong for so long ere the mask cracks and reveals the truth. Now will you come? I will bear you to them."

Hadriel nodded, slowly at first, and then with decision. She climbed onto the scaled back of the Serpent and perched at the base of his long neck. He dropped into the water and glided toward the peasants in the bay.

A rumble of thunder heralded the belated arrival of the storm. Black clouds unleashed a torrent of rain as the voyagers scrambled to find a position on the Serpent's back. He pushed off from shore and sailed across the Loch, body twisting through the pounding waves.

The Kingdom faded from sight behind them.

Hadriel closed her eyes and lifted her face to the gale.

She was free.

*****

"Arise, little one." The Serpent's neck twisted to look at her, huddled close to the welcome heat radiating from the cracks between his scales. "Behold the Island."

The vibrations of his voice rumbled along his iron-ridged back and into Hadriel's fingers. She stood, balancing gingerly with one hand against his upraised neck. Water droplets settled on her eyelashes as she peered into the mist.

A shadow appeared ahead, like a thick bank of fog. It loomed larger as the Serpent approached, sharpening into the distinct form of a shore that vanished into the mist a few yards above the tide line.

Laughter welled in Hadriel's chest at the sight. She hugged the Serpent's neck and then jerked away, breath quickening at her own daring. But he did not rebuke her. He slowed and came to a gentle stop, rocking on the incoming waves. Muted sounds filled the air: a baby's cry, the shrill chatter of children, and the rumble of muttered conversations lost and jumbled in the enveloping cloud.

A man's familiar voice grumbled behind Hadriel. "Cursed fog. Where are the so-called wonders of this place? Can't see much of anything now, can we?"

"Not if you just sit there, Hoag." She tossed her hair back from her face and peered at the dark water, gauging the depth. It seemed shallow enough. "I, for one, intend to go ashore." She dropped from the Serpent's back and slid into waist-deep water.

The cold tore her breath away. Shivering, she gathered her skirt in one hand and waded toward dry land. She paused just beyond the waterline and turned back to the peasants clinging to the Serpent's back.

"What are you waiting for? We're here. Come on!"

Still they lingered.

Hadriel shook her head in disgust as she wrung the water from her skirt and rubbed the feeling back into limbs numbed by the Loch's chill. They were fools to be frightened *now,* after daring so much and coming so far.

Yet why should she care?

The Island *was* real, and it was hers for the taking.

She turned in search of the wonders the Serpent had described and caught just a glimpse of his expression. His mouth cracked into a jagged smile, and there was a fiendish glint in his eyes. Cries split the air as the Serpent submerged and shot into deeper water, leaving his passengers afloat. Hadriel stifled a laugh when Hoag surfaced, spluttering and bellowing, water dribbling from his beard. Amidst a flurry of complaints, the new arrivals floundered to rescue their bundles and scramble to shore.

Hadriel ventured inland, rough black rock stabbing her bare feet. She gazed into the swirling mist and begged the fog to clear. It veiled the wonders of the Island as surely as the King's command had concealed its existence. To think that she had come so far, forsaking the Kingdom and daring the King's wrath, only to be cheated from the sight of the ultimate reward. She swallowed the frustration rising in her throat.

A loud shriek rang out behind.

Heart beating wildly, she spun around, ignoring the pain of sharp rocks slicing into her heels. Eyes blazing in triumph, the Serpent lifted his craggy head to the skies. He screeched again then lunged into the deep and vanished beneath the foaming waters of the Loch.

Hadriel froze. Terror struck the pit of her stomach, followed by a horrible sense of loss and fear. Something was wrong. Terribly wrong.

She noticed a gradual change in the mist. Dim gray light grew around her. A bitter wind stirred over the silent island, lifting the hair plastered to her scalp, drifting beneath the layers of her wet skirt, and shredding the tendrils of fog.

Her lungs burned and she realized that she had almost forgotten to breathe since landing. She gulped in a shuddering breath and gagged at the foul smell borne upon the wind, but for a moment she was thankful. At last she would be able to see the marvels of the Island.

The final threads of fog scattered before the strengthening breeze, revealing her surroundings. Hadriel's mouth dropped open. A cry froze on her lips as she fell to her knees.

No paradise met her eyes, no land glowing with light or teeming with life. This was a place of death and darkness—a bare black rock that pierced the turbulent waters of the Loch as the tip of a mountain breaks through surrounding clouds. Craggy boulders dotted the barren landscape, haphazardly joined by stunted thorn trees and twisted bushes wreathed in sharp spines. Cold wind wrapped around the Island, ceaselessly sighing over the deserted rocks and desolate shore.

"No!" Hadriel choked on the word. Staggering to her feet, she stumbled past the stunned peasants to the Loch and collapsed in the shallows.

Far across the water, the Kingdom appeared little more than a glimpse of green on the horizon between deep water and midnight sky. So far away... too far and too late to turn back now. Confused shouting and wailing broke out behind her. She groaned, clasped her hands to her ears to block the cries, and rocked back and forth in silent agony.

What have I done?

Then all other sounds faded before the rumble of a deep, familiar voice. "Dear ones..."

Hadriel's skin turned to ice. How many times had she heard that voice and welcomed the sound with joy? Now it filled her with shame. Her heart ached as if pierced by a dozen swords. The urge to flee and seek a place to hide tugged at her limbs, but instead, she rose and slowly turned around.

White light met her eyes, painfully bright compared to the surrounding gloom. Somewhere in the midst of the glow was a figure—that of the King, she knew—but her eyes burned at the brightness and she could not bear to look. She glanced down, down into darkness to ease the pain.

The King must have discovered their flight and followed them in his swift white ship to this forbidden place. But had he come to offer rescue or enact terrible vengeance for their disobedience?

She trembled at the thought.

The King began to speak to the peasants, but his words resonated so within her soul that it seemed he spoke to her alone. "What did you lack, little one? Of what were you in need? Tell me what injustice I have done, what trials I have heaped upon you, or what oppression I have caused. Did I not freely provide all you needed? Why did you follow the Serpent and forsake my Kingdom?"

"You deceived us," Hoag shouted. "You hid your knowledge from us."

The King's wrath seemed to grow like a heavy weight on the air. "I told you all you needed to know."

Hadriel opened her mouth to speak, but no words surfaced. A deep sob shook her frame as the truth of the Serpent's betrayal played out in her mind. "The Serpent lied to us!" And then she faltered. Deep within, she knew that the blame for her decision rested on her and her alone. She had chosen to follow the Serpent—chosen to believe his lies and reject the King.

The burden of the thought drove her to her knees. "Please, have mercy." She struggled to raise her head, her gaze traveling from the King's boots up the dusty train of his robe to the brilliant sword belted at his side. "Forgive us, O King." Her gaze halted at the golden beard splayed across his chest like an inverted crown. She could not bring herself to meet his eyes.

"Attend to me." The sternness of his voice sent a fresh blade of sorrow through Hadriel's heart. "Because you listened to the Serpent and chose his way over mine, you will follow him and live as you longed to live." His judgment fell on her ears like the harsh clanging of a hammer against a bell. As he spoke, mist filled her vision.

The seasons churned before her eyes: summer wasting away into autumn and winter—a lengthy winter followed by a short spring.

"The years will pass. You will scratch out your living on this accursed rock."

Begrimed peasants, crippled with labor, bent over a patch of soil chipped from stone. Scattered implements, fallen from weary hands, lined the rows of pale green shoots. A howling wind barreled through, threatening to tear the struggling crop from the earth.

"You will toil for every scrap of food you eat."

Twin red orbs blazed out of suffocating blackness. A strange gravity settled around her, sucking her toward the fire fueling the Serpent's eyes.

Hadriel cried out and tried to pull away.

"You will dwell under the fear of the Serpent all the days of your life."

A sob caught in her throat. Dimly she heard the cries of the peasants begging for mercy. She raised trembling hands to her mouth, but her voice had fled. *Mercy. Please, have mercy!*

"You have heard the curse." The King's voice softened. "Now hear the promise." As he studied the crowd, Hadriel's gaze, previously fixed on his beard, was drawn to his eyes—purest blue surrounded by a crown of smile lines that now drooped in sorrow. A boundless flood of pity, grief, and wrath teemed in the depths of his timeless gaze.

"I will not forget you. Though you have disobeyed me and forsaken me, I will remember you. One day, in the midst of the darkness, a light will come, and innocent blood will pay the price of the faithless."

Radiance flooded her vision.

An echoing shriek, a roar of fury, a sword bathed in brilliant light, and the silhouette of a man standing with arms outstretched.

Gray spun over her eyes and she bowed her head. When she finally looked about, the light had dwindled; the King was gone. The villagers stood alone on the barren shore with dark waves crashing around them. Far to her right, Hadriel caught sight of a single white ship cutting through the water. The King stood in the stern, deep in conversation with a man who was hooded and cloaked.

As the man looked back across the intervening water, a gust of wind tore his hood aside. It was the Prince. He gazed intently at the Island, determination etched in his face, his hand grasping the hilt of his sword.

Then he turned away.

Hadriel longed to call out, but the cry lodged in her chest. The ship scudded across the Loch and in but a few moments, disappeared from sight. A dark mist rose from the water, filling the air with the reek of death. Fog wrapped around the Island, shielding the horizon and any glimpse of the Kingdom from view.

Tears came to Hadriel's eyes. She knelt on the stones and wept bitterly.

PART TWO

The Shadow of Death

Drums.

Drums beating in the darkness.

Marya shuddered and wrapped her arms around her knees. *Death – death – death*, the drums seemed to chant. Orange lights flickered beneath the wooden door and through the chinks in the walls, drawing nearer.

Across the room, her parents' cot rustled and she heard the soft mumble of their voices—her mother's tone rising in anxiety, and her father's deep, reassuring rumble.

"It's all right," he soothed.

But when had it ever been all right?

"Has it always been this way?" The half-whispered words echoed bitterly in her mind. It was said that there had been a time, long ago, when the villagers were but peasants, happy and free, a time when they dwelt in a kingdom ruled by a kind and mighty King, a time when they knew nothing of fear or terror or death. So it was said—but such a thing seemed impossible. Could there ever have truly been a time when the villagers were free from the terror of the Serpent and the rule of the Tribunal?

Only fools believed the old tales. Only fools sought hope while awaiting death at the claws of the Serpent. Like doddering ancients grasping blindly at fairy tales, her parents clung to whispered legends of the King and his forgotten promise.

Fairy tales—that's all they were. Nothing else.

"Fairy tales," she whispered savagely into the darkness.

Closer and closer the drums sounded, deafening, aching, pounding. Her head hammered, throbbing in rhythm until the relentless beat swallowed her. She clutched the blanket to her chest and slid back on her cot until her back pressed against the stone wall.

They were coming.

A thunderous rumbling shook the door, and the drums fell silent.

Marya held her breath. The chill wind wailed perpetually past the hut, whistling through the crevices in the walls. A wolf howled in the distance. Footsteps crunched against gravel followed by a rap on the door—a hollow sound in the small hut.

"Father?" her voice wavered.

"Stay there, Marya." The cot creaked as he rose, and his feet thudded across the packed dirt floor. She heard the sharp *tck-tck* of flint striking steel; a tiny tongue of flame darted to a torch in his hand.

The torch flared to life, casting shadows across his grim face as he stepped toward the door. He reached above the doorframe and pulled down his axe. Voices clamored outside, a confused babble of shouts and angry cries. The door trembled beneath repeated strokes, hinges groaning and planks splintering.

Marya turned to her mother.

Ayanna sat up in bed, clutching her shawl, her face paler than the moonlight creeping through the thatched roof. "Corridan, don't!" Her hair, the same streaked ashen blonde as Marya's, tumbled in wild waves around her face. She scrambled from bed and grabbed Corridan's outstretched hand. "Don't answer it."

"I have to."

"Not this way." She laid her hand on the axe. "Never this way."

Corridan set her aside and pressed the torch into her hands. "I will protect my family." Hefting the axe in one hand, he reached for the bolt with the other.

The door burst from its hinges.

Corridan pulled Ayanna out of the way as splintered wood crashed to the floor and orange light flooded the hut. He stepped into the doorway, squaring his broad shoulders. "Maddrel?" His voice thundered out. "Where are you? Come forth and answer me. Why do you disturb peaceful villagers in the dead of night?"

Silence fell, more sinister than the angry shouts of a moment before.

Crouched in the corner, Marya peered through the crook of her arm at the open doorway. Torches blazed in the hands of the mob surrounding the hut, and spearheads glinted like spurts of flame at the end of their long staffs. The intruders were clad in ragged black robes and haunting white masks marked with the figure of a charcoal-colored serpent wreathed in red flames.

The Tribunal—such a visit could mean only one thing.

"It is time." The ranks of the Tribunal parted and Maddrel stepped forward. The silver snakelike emblem coiled on the front of his black robe proclaimed his status as high priest.

"Time for what?" Corridan settled the axe on his shoulder where the threat was clearly visible to all.

"The culling. Word has reached the Tribunal that you follow the way of fools as your ancestors did, that you do not acknowledge the rule of the Serpent, that you believe in the tales of a King and his promises." Maddrel spat and stepped to Corridan's side, black robe swishing like the decaying wings of a carrion bird. "The Tribunal has called you and your wife to the place of Rahedhenaur."

More quickly than Marya could follow, Corridan darted to the left, swung the axe from his shoulder, and hooked the haft around Maddrel's neck, clenching the priest in a death grip. The muscles bulged on his arms and neck. "Send your servants away, priest, or you will meet the Serpent yourself."

Maddrel clawed feebly at Corridan's hands. A strangled cough burst from his throat. He managed to tug the handle away from his neck long enough to rasp, "Resist and you will *all* die."

The Tribunal lifted their torches to the roof and paused with the flames licking at the thatching. Marya's stomach churned, and she suppressed the urge to bolt to her feet, break through the mob, and flee to the hills. Flight was a vain hope. She would not be able to escape if the Tribunal desired her death.

"Surrender and your daughter goes free."

"Free?" Corridan began, but his voice caught. "What is freedom here?" He looked back over his shoulder at Marya—never before had she seen him appear so helpless and torn. His expression shifted and resignation dulled his gaze.

She staggered to her feet. "No, Father. Don't!"

The axe dropped from his hands, blade cleaving the earth at his feet. Corridan released Maddrel and shoved him toward the rest of the Tribunal. Lowering his head, he held out his arms. "So be it."

"Take him!" Maddrel screamed.

The priests swarmed Corridan, seizing his arms and leading him, unresisting, into the night.

"No!" The cry burst from Marya's lips, echoed by her mother. She shoved past the startled priests, somehow evading their grasp, and raced to Corridan. "Father, no."

For a moment, he broke free and hugged her. She clutched his shoulder, burying her face against his arm. It felt as though a giant hand squeezed her throat until tears blurred her vision but she could not cry out. Something wet splashed on her forearm; she looked up to see tears in Corridan's eyes.

"Marya, all will be well." He kissed her on the top of her head—just as he had done since she was a child. Hard hands grasped her shoulders and wrenched her away.

She hit the earth hard. Pain surged through her head at the jolt and she blinked to clear her vision. Maddrel loomed over her. The hideous white mask sucked in toward his face as he breathed; black-ringed holes, like the empty sockets of a skull, leered down at her.

"The man and his wife will go to the Rahedhenaur," he intoned. "Let the girl witness the power of the Serpent—she may yet be reclaimed from their poisonous ways." He flicked a lazy hand, sending two more priests into the hut. They emerged a moment later with Ayanna held tightly between them.

"Mother!"

Ayanna stretched an arm out to Marya and called her name, but the Tribunal yanked her away. Maddrel motioned the procession forward. As the column marched off, one of the priests blew a long blast on a curved sea horn. Dull and harsh, the call blasted across the Island, ordering all the villagers to the Rahedhenaur.

The drums began and the line of torches moved on. Marya followed, tears falling steadily from her eyes. Twice a month, the Serpent chose a sacrifice from among the villagers. Twice a month, all were summoned to the Rahedhenaur to await his choice. Such was life on the Island. Always the threat loomed in the distance—the fear that perhaps this time a loved one would be called to the Stone. Sooner or later, all the villagers would stand before the Serpent. Old and young, weak and strong. It was inevitable.

But the last choosing had been scarce a week ago. Marya hugged her arms to her chest. They *should* have been safe if not for the culling... if only her parents had not fallen prey to the hopeless delusions of their long-dead ancestors.

The Tribunal hunted any villagers who refused to worship the Serpent or preached belief in the ancient myths—hunted and dragged them to the Stone where they were offered as an additional blood-gift to appease the Island's voracious master.

There was no escape.

The drumbeat pounded in Marya's mind, matching the steady tramping of her feet.

Death – death – death.

*****

"Silence, all, to hear the proceedings of the Tribunal." Maddrel's voice blared beside Marya's ear. The drums fell silent, and the drone of voices died away until all was still, save the wind.

Marya shivered—as much from fear as from the cold. Water dripped from the ragged hem of her skirt, the drops trailing down her legs before plopping to the Stone below. Angry waves, lashed with foam, crashed against the flat-topped boulder beneath her feet. It jutted out of the water like a tiny island in the midst of a raging sea.

About twenty yards of restless water surged between the Stone and the shore where the entire village gathered inside the jagged columns of black rock which formed the circle of Rahedhenaur. Marya sensed their terror as they waited in trembling rows. They were right to be afraid. Though it was but the culling and not the usual day for sacrifice, none could say who else the Serpent might choose that day.

The Rahedhenaur stood like a darker blotch in the center of that barren shoreline beneath the shadow of jagged black hills. How many times had she stood within that circle, dreading the day when she or her parents would be called to the Stone?

Now it had come.

Eyes fixed on the boulder beneath her feet, she clutched a hand to her mouth to hold back the tide of sickness rising in her throat. A black and crimson film streaked the surface of the rock. The Stone was stained with the blood of countless villagers murdered to appease the Serpent's bloodlust and slake his insatiable appetite. A groan swelled in her throat, and she did not try to suppress it.

"Bring forth the prisoners to stand before the Tribunal."

The drums began again—the same, slow, throbbing beat. Two priests emerged from the circle and slowly marched across the beach and down into the water. Behind them, Marya caught a glimpse of her parents, followed by two more priests. Ayanna stumbled as she walked, leaning heavily on Corridan's arm. Her face was white and her eyes were wide with fear. But no fear marred Corridan's expression, though his wrists were bound. Shoulders back, head erect, he walked to his doom as steadily as if he were on his way to work in the fields.

Marya gulped back a sob as they reached the Stone, and one by one all six clambered to the top and halted before Maddrel.

The high priest clasped his hands before him. "Corridan and Ayanna, you have been called to the Rahedhenaur by the culling to await the judgment of the Serpent. You stand accused of refusing to submit to the rule of the Serpent and persisting in the foolish belief of a legendary king. The Serpent will decide your fate. But first, you have one last chance to bend knee to our lord and master. What say you?" He waited, and then repeated the question, louder. "What say you? Will you recant?"

Corridan yanked free and stepped forward, determination written on his face. "I will not."

The priests seized him and shoved him back.

Maddrel's breath hissed through the gaping mouthpiece of the mask. "Then by your own tongue you have sealed your fate. Those who refuse allegiance to the Serpent will die."

"No, please!" Marya cried out. Without so much as a glance at her, Maddrel backhanded her across the face. She stumbled back, cheek and mouth burning. Blood trickled from her lip and dropped onto her hand.

Maddrel hovered over Ayanna, speaking in a low voice. "Your husband has made his decision. You must make yours. Think of your daughter. What will become of her after you are both slain? Would you doom her to a life of starvation and poverty? Outcast from the villagers. Forsaken. Alone."

Marya could see the inner combat reflected in Ayanna's eyes. "Don't leave. Please don't leave me." *Not alone. Not an outcast. Say yes,* she pleaded silently. *Forget about the legends and remember me.*

Ayanna's lips trembled and she closed her eyes. Tears rolled freely down her face. Maddrel lingered at her elbow. Though the mask hid his features from view, he obviously relished the pain and suffering he inflicted. At last, Ayanna raised her head and steadily met Maddrel's gaze. Her voice quavered as she spoke, but the torment was gone from her eyes.

"I have only this to say," she said, her voice growing in firmness and volume, as though she gathered strength from her own confession. "There is a King. He has promised to return. He will come and rescue us. I will never bow to the Serpent or acknowledge his lordship."

"Foolish woman!" Maddrel shook his fist in her face, emphasizing his every word. "There is no king, no promise, no rescue. There is only the Serpent." He rushed to the shoreward edge of the Stone and motioned to the villagers assembled in the circle. "Ask them," he shouted. "Ask any of them—from the most ancient elder to the youngest babe—and they will tell you that the Serpent alone rules. Your *king* does not exist."

Spurred by the Tribunal, the villagers took up the cry until it reverberated from the hills. "The Serpent rules. The Serpent is lord."

Maddrel turned back to face Corridan and Ayanna, arms lifted to the sky. "The Serpent is lord," he repeated. And as his eyes shifted past them to the Loch, he fell silent. Dread settled on Marya like an icy hand gripping her heart in its cruel fingers. She struggled to breathe. The ghastly white mask grinned and Maddrel spoke again. "The Serpent has come."

Marya's eyes followed Maddrel's pointing finger. Night had broken. A thin line of gray crept across the eastern sky, the first fingers of dawn. The ceremonial proceedings of the Tribunal had consumed the predawn hours, and now a strange, thick, roiling blackness approached from the south, speeding toward the Island on the wings of a storm. It settled overhead; Marya blinked to readjust her eyes.

A white line appeared in the corner of her vision, a crest of water sweeping across the Loch and approaching the shore with terrifying rapidity. The wave swelled as it neared and crashed against the shore. Utter stillness fell.

Marya's mouth went dry and her legs trembled.

The Loch heaved and the Serpent surfaced. His hideous head shot out first, followed by yard after yard of sinuous neck and two mighty forearms. The priest to Marya's right raised the sea horn to his lips and blew a long blast that resounded from the surrounding crescent of hills. Beside her, Maddrel dropped to his knees and bowed his masked head to the ground.

Before Marya had time to think or react, she was shoved down next to him. She landed heavily on the sharp stones, biting her lip in the fall. Heavy hands remained on her shoulders, holding her in place so that she could not rise, even if she had desired to.

Grunting and stamping feet broke out behind her. One of the priests stumbled over her, and then rose, cursing. Marya looked over her shoulder. Corridan stood, steady and firm as the Stone itself, resisting the efforts of the priests to pull him to his knees beside Ayanna.

Maddrel raised his head, anger so contorting his features that Marya could see it through his mask. "Be quick, you fools. The prisoner may not remain standing before the Serpent."

The Tribunal redoubled their efforts, no doubt goaded by fear of Maddrel as much as of the Serpent. A flurry of blows broke out—the wet thud of punches and the resounding crack of striking staffs—and Corridan collapsed beneath the fury of the priests. He lay unmoving, cheek pressed flat against the Stone, blood dripping from a deep cut on his forehead to pool on the crimson rock. Two priests knelt on either side, pinning him down.

Marya turned away, blinking through her tears.

The Serpent drew nearer and halted with his claws only a few feet from the Stone. His great head towered high above. Smoke billowed as he opened his mouth, revealing a double set of jagged fangs. Red fire burned in the depths of his throat, reflecting off his fangs so that they too appeared to be covered in blood. The air, bitterly cold a moment before, now felt dry and hot as though the Serpent had sucked all of the moisture from the sky.

He spoke. His voice seemed to come from a great depth, grating and rumbling like the clatter of falling stones. "Corridan and Ayanna, foolish ones. There is no king. I rule—I alone. I decide your fate. You will hail me as king. All will acknowledge me or perish."

Corridan spat blood. Still half-dazed, he struggled to rise, but the priests held him fast. "Serpent," he spoke between clenched teeth, "you are a deceiver! You bring death to all. We will never acknowledge your reign. There is only one King and he yet lives. He will return and when he does, you will be defeated and—"

The Serpent screeched. The flames smoldering in his throat sprang to life and shot into the air. Priests dove out of the way as the Serpent's head flashed down—once, twice.

A scream ripped from Marya's throat as Corridan and Ayanna crumpled beneath the Serpent's onslaught. "Father! Mother! No!" She struggled against the tight grip that held her down, fighting and screaming with all of her might.

Wham. Something hard hit her in the back and she fell, skidding across the wet rock. Her head smashed against the Stone, and pain exploded within her skull.

Golden lights burst across her vision, casting a hazy glow over her surroundings. Her body felt strangely weightless as if she were going to float away, but her head seemed heavy, dragging her down again. A torrential roar of meaningless noise rang in her ears.

Through the haze, Marya watched the Serpent's clawed hands reach down and grasp the two limp forms, lifting them from the rock. His gaze traveled back to the shore where the frightened villagers waited in the Rahedhenaur. "These traitors are the only ones I will take today."

The tension in the crowd eased, washing back across the Loch like a breath of wind.

The Serpent held up the bloodied bodies of Corridan and Ayanna so that all could see. "Beware that you do not follow the traitor's way. It is the way of death."

A cry answered from the circle, "The Serpent rules."

Once more, the villagers broke into the chant.

Marya reeled to her feet as the Serpent drifted away. "Take me," she screamed. "Take me too!"

His neck swayed back until his head stooped even with hers. Heat blazed from his eyes—deep red pools of burning liquid that relentlessly drew her gaze inward. Smoke engulfed her as the Serpent spoke. "Sssoon enough, little one." His bloodstained mouth warped into a crooked smile. Then he twisted around and plunged into the Loch, taking Corridan and Ayanna to the deep.

Numbness drifted over her. She dropped to her knees, gazing at the widening rings crawling across the Loch from the place where the Serpent had submerged. The horizon spun before her eyes, tilting first one direction then the other. She realized that she had not wept since the Serpent arrived; now she found she could not. Her throat ached with a lump of pent-up sorrow waiting to be released, but no tears came. Dry, shuddering sobs shook her body.

Mother, Father—the names froze on her tongue, refusing to be spoken. They were gone. Taken by the Serpent. And for what? Fairy tales. A King who had not saved them. A promise unfulfilled. "Why?" The words burst through her clenched teeth. "Why?"

At last the tears surfaced, streaming down her cheeks and splashing onto the blood-soaked rock. Marya lowered her head into her hands and sobbed.

*****

Marya stood stiffly and wiped her face with an already soaked sleeve. How long had she lain there? Eventide hung heavy over the Island. Pale light filtered through the fog on the western horizon—the sun was about to set. She stood alone on the Stone, and the Rahedhenaur lay in uneasy slumber behind her, once more deserted by the villagers until the Serpent's return.

She winced as she took a step toward the edge. Every muscle ached and her head throbbed persistently. Movement caught her eye as she turned—something fluttering on the far side of the Stone. A dark blue strip of fabric dangled in the wind. Marya scrambled to the edge and caught the cloth before the wind dragged it away. Her mother's shawl.

Hugging it to her chest, she slipped over the side and fled to the empty shore. Halting as she reached firm ground, Marya looked back across the water to the Stone glinting blood red in the dim light. She wrapped the shawl around her shoulders and clutched the ends in both hands, nestling into its comforting warmth.

Ducking her head as the tears began to flow again, Marya dashed across the shore and over the rock-strewn hillside toward home. Her steps slowed as the familiar path drew her near to the stone hut where she had lived her entire life. How could she go on? The hut would seem so empty and frightening now, haunted by memories that were crueler than the Serpent's claws. But there was nowhere else to go. Maddrel had seen to that.

As the daughter of traitors, she was truly and totally alone. No outcast was allowed in the village, nor were any villagers permitted to offer aid or comfort to an exile. Outcasts often fled to the barren hills on the far side of the Island, but she could not join them there. Even they would be sure to shun her for her parents' beliefs.

Dragging her feet, Marya rounded the last bend in the well-known path and burst out running, sudden horror lending speed to her legs. Their hut was gone. A pile of smoke-blackened rubble squatted in its place. Small pockets of flame licked at the fallen wooden beams that once supported the thatched roof, while the walls had been torn down and shattered as if a giant hand had smashed into them. Was there nothing sacred? Could they not have left her with even a vestige of her parents' lives?

Weighed down by this last, dreadful blow, Marya sank to the ground and dug her fists into the earth. Something cold and wet landed on her neck. Towering black clouds swept across the sky, swollen and threatening rain. A clap of thunder sounded out, the clouds tore open, and rain poured from the sky. Marya huddled into a ball, hugging her knees and ducking her head between her arms. The merciless rain pounded the back of her neck. She watched through a curtain of her own tangled hair as the rain squelched the last fires, flames fizzling out into a cloud of blue smoke.

Marya tugged the shawl over her head and lay down on the wet ground, too spent to seek cover. She closed her eyes in a vain search for sleep, but the Serpent's gaze haunted her dreams. Thunder rumbled in the distance and she started up, gasping for breath, thinking she heard his voice again.

Sssoon enough, little one.

Once more, she saw her parents fall before his onslaught—bodies broken, blood pooling on the stone. Slain for a lie. "Why... why did you do it?" A flash of lightning crawled across the sky and she struggled to her feet amidst the pelting rain and screamed to the sky. "If there is a King, he failed you. He failed me! What of the promise now?"

The wind lashed the rain into her eyes. Blinded, Marya fell back and lay with her cheek pressed to the cold, wet earth. She sighed, a deep shuddering sigh. At last she had the answer. "There is no King," she whispered into the darkness. "No rescue. No promise. The Serpent rules."

PART THREE

Dawning

One year later

Marya's breath misted before her eyes as she dropped into a crouch behind a boulder and peered over the crest of the hill. Late autumn's chill had seized the Island with damp, frostbitten fingers that chapped her cheeks, gnawed at her bones and left her longing for the warmth of a hearth and home.

Smoke rose from the village, a cluster of buildings dotting the rocky plateau opposite her. Villagers bustled through the streets with chins tucked against the wind or darted in and out of shop doorways. Here and there, she spied the dark shapes of Tribunal priests cleaving a wide path through the crowd. Instinctively, she flattened herself against the hillside, recalling her first and last entry into the village after her parents' death a year past. Curses, stones and the priests' staffs had greeted her—followed by threats of worse punishment should she ever return.

She had a different objective in mind today. Her gaze traveled to the small field sprawled in the trough between her hill and the plateau. Furrows curved across the field to avoid the large outcropping of rock at the base of her hill. At the far end of the field, a farmer and two lads, who looked too much like him to be anything but his sons, toiled with hoes.

Familiar faces—she must have "visited" them at least a dozen times over the course of the past year, each time growing a trifle bolder than before. But their wariness had grown to match her courage since the time she had made off with a hammer, hoe, and sack of food all in the same afternoon. She would have to be careful.

Once she must have known their names, but now she could not recall them, nor did she care to try to remember. She was nothing more than an outcast to them, so let them be nothing more than unwitting and unwilling suppliers to her. In the end, it made no difference. Preoccupied with work, they would neither see nor hear her. Sly as a wolf, she would attack and be gone before the first cry of alarm.

One learned much about the arts of stealth and thievery in a year of exile. It was the only way to survive.

On silent feet, she crept down the hill and skidded to a stop behind the outcrop. A peek around the side revealed the farmer and his sons still hard at work. Clutching the rock, she hoisted herself up to perch on the edge. There it was—

the object that had drawn her down from the hills—a brown sack slouching on the top of the rock to her right. The aroma emanating from within set her head spinning with hunger.

Her fingers trembled as she fumbled with the cords, then she yanked the sack open and peered inside. *Glories!* A whole meat pie. She turned to descend and her foot knocked a broken chunk of rock to the ground with a *clunk* that set her hair on end.

"Hoi! Stop it!" the farmer shouted. "You pesky wretch, get away from our food."

Marya jolted, cursing her own clumsiness. Her foot slipped and she fell, still clutching the sack. By the time she regained her breath enough to rise, the farmer and his sons were halfway across the field.

She broke into a run, hugging the precious pie to her chest. A rock flew past her head and thudded into the hillside. Up and over the hill she raced, picking up speed on the descent until it seemed she had grown wings and would lift from the earth at any moment. The wind surged in her face and she flung her head back.

Here, on the run, she came alive. Alive as she had not been since her parents' death.

As she started up the next slope, she risked a glance back over her shoulder. The portly farmer had already begun to fall behind, red-faced and shouting as he stumbled and listed from side to side with every step. But his sons raced on, fleet-footed as ever, closing the gap.

Marya set her teeth. Once they had almost caught her. Only the onset of night and the howling of wolves in the hills had turned them from her trail. She could not let it come so close again.

Not going to catch me. Not this time!

At the foot of the hill, the ground leveled and she settled into her fastest pace, arms and legs pumping. A jumbled mass of broken rock fingers stabbed up from the ground to her right, and she altered course to meet it—the Stone Forest. There among the rocks, she could lose them.

She darted into the rocks, circling, dodging, and twisting around thick trunks of stone that towered above her head. At last she collapsed, panting, in the gap between two fallen stones. The farmer's sons were nowhere to be seen.

With a grin clinging to her lips, Marya peeled the sack away from the pie. Thick brown gravy oozed through the broken crust. She sniffed, closing her eyes to savor the smell. With any luck the farmer's sons were too far behind to catch the scent. Throwing manners to the wind, Marya dug into the pie, palming huge chunks of crust and meat into her mouth and licking the sticky sauce from her fingers.

A meal prepared for three men working in the fields meant *she* would have plenty to last through the next day. One less meal to scavenge for. One more day to survive.

At last, she wiped her hands on her skirt and wrapped the remainder of the pie in the borrowed sack. She emerged from her hiding place into the dull silver of dusk and suppressed a tremor of fear at the looming shadows. Surely it could not be so late already! Darkness would overtake her long before she reached home, and wild beasts were always on the prowl beneath the cover of night's shade.

Heedless now of the mild threat posed by the farmers, Marya hurried back through the Stone Forest and jogged south toward the shore and home. Evening slipped into night as she ran, cursing her own forgetfulness. A full moon filtered white light through shreds of swirling mist, highlighting her path. Rising hillocks and jagged rocks showed up black against the hazy landscape. A high-pitched quavering cry broke the silence to her left, and an answering call sounded from just behind.

Marya froze, her muscles taut. The cries sounded again—closer—mournful, undulating howls. Wolves. She caught sight of them dashing toward her through the mist, flying burs of bluish-white fur and gleaming teeth.

She fled, stretching to the utmost until she feared her muscles would tear with the strain. A wolf snapped at her heels. It missed, but only by a fraction. Another caught the hem of her skirt in its teeth. The fabric ripped and Marya pulled free, falling forward to land on her hands and knees in the dirt. The sack flew from her hand and vanished in the night. Snarling, the wolves leapt upon her.

Pain ripped through her ankle and she kicked out, detaching the wolf from her leg. A hideous head loomed over her, pale luminous eyes fixed on her own. Saliva dripped on her neck as the wolf bared its teeth for the lunge.

Thud. The wolf yelped and toppled over, paws scrabbling to find a purchase. Flames smoldered in the silver fur on its side.

"Look out!" a voice shouted.

Marya looked up as a third wolf charged. Its teeth sank into her right arm, opening a jagged crimson line before she managed to kick it away. Defensively, she curled into a ball, arms wrapped around her head.

A shadowed figure leapt between her and the circling wolves. Swinging a burning brand around his head until he appeared to be wreathed in fire, the man steadily approached the ravenous animals. They backed away, whimpering, then overcome by bloodlust, one jumped at his throat. The stranger halted the beast with a well-placed kick and downward swipe of the torch. The wolf yelped and fled, blood dripping from its flaming muzzle.

The other two wolves were more cunning—one darting in to snap at the man's legs, while the other diverted his attention. The noise of combat filled the air, a horrendous cacophony of grunts, shrieks, and the rush of flames.

"Run, Marya," the stranger commanded. "Run!"

Marya lurched to her feet. Risking a last glance behind—the stranger seemed to be holding his own for the moment—she tore off across the hillside, clutching her injured arm to her chest, howls still ringing in her ears.

*****

Home at last, Marya stumbled into the pathetic shelter she had managed to build from the piles of rubble. One of the corners of the hut had survived the Tribunal's fury, and about five feet of wall on either side of the corner still stood waist-high. Dried rushes stretched over the corner served as her roof, a poor protection against the cold and none at all against the rain. She had tried to pile up broken rocks to fill in the gap between the two walls, but for the most part the third side was still exposed to the elements. The triangular shelter offered just enough room to crawl into at night and sleep with at least the illusion of protection from wild beasts in the dark.

A shudder seized her, and she hugged her arms in a vain attempt to relieve the chill. If the stranger had not appeared to rescue her, she would already be dead—perhaps *he* was dead, and it was her fault for so foolishly venturing across the Island in the dark when the beasts prowled.

No, it was not her fault. It was just this place.

This place where death reigned.

With practiced callousness, she pushed the thought from her mind and stoked her dying fire to life, adding wood until the flames blazed. It should be enough to keep the wolves away if she awoke often enough to keep it lit through the long hours of the night. Exhausted, she tumbled into her straw bed, pulled her knotted waves of hair into a loose braid, curled beneath Ayanna's shawl, and closed her eyes.

Flashing teeth hung over her face. She looked up past the dark cavity of the wolf's yawning throat and saw death— her death—in its eyes.

"Sssoon, little one."

But the beast suddenly collapsed, and a dark figure leaped between her and the wolves. He spoke without turning to face her. "Run, Marya! Run."

She reeled to her feet, gasping for breath, and hugged Ayanna's shawl to her chest. How had he known her name?

*****

Marya shivered awake to the first light of dawn falling through the open side of her shelter. She rubbed the last shades of sleep from her eyes and winced as she stretched. The angry red cuts on her arm and ankle throbbed—she would have to clean them later or risk infection. She could almost hear Ayanna scolding her for not bothering to clean them before falling asleep, and the thought brought a sad smile to her lips.

Slinging the shawl around her shoulders, Marya ducked out of the shelter and straightened slowly, rubbing her hands together to restore feeling to her numb fingers. She kicked at the cold pile of charred sticks, scattering dead ashes over the ground. The fire had gone out, and she, fool that she was, had not awakened to tend it.

At least the wolves had not returned.

"Good morning."

She spun around at the unexpected voice, heart hammering in her chest so she could scarce hear her own words. "Who's there?"

"Don't be afraid. I won't harm you."

Marya spied the owner of the voice sitting a few paces from her shelter, back toward her, arms resting on his raised knees. He was dressed in rags nearly as tattered as her own and had a tightly wrapped bundle bound to his back with a braided cord.

Was it the farmer? Or one of the many others who had unwillingly contributed food over the past few months? She dropped to one knee, scanning the surrounding area, and scooped up a fist-sized rock. The intruder seemed to be alone, but others could well be hidden among the scattered rocks.

After a moment of silence and stillness, she took a deep breath. "What do you want?"

"I *want* nothing." He turned his head to look at her. Light hair hung across his forehead and stuck out in all directions like uneven thatching. His face was unfamiliar. She had certainly never stolen from him. Still, his voice…

"You are the stranger. You rescued me from the wolves."

He tilted his head in acknowledgment. "You should not wander alone after dark. Why do you live out here in the ruins and not in the village? You would be safer there."

"Not all the wolves on the Island dwell in the hills." She folded her arms and studied the stranger. "I am safer among the wild beasts."

He met her gaze, unflinching beneath her scrutiny. If he was but a piece in a trap, then it was a good one. Yet what else could it be? No villager would dare speak to an outcast lest the judgment of the Tribunal fall upon them. But why had he saved her from the wolves if he meant her harm?

"Why are you here? Surely you know the penalty for aiding an outcast. You must leave before it is too late."

The man simply shrugged his shoulders. "I am a stranger here. Tell me the penalty."

His casual manner chilled her.

"Death," she whispered. "The penalty is death."

The stranger whistled through his teeth. "That's quite a severe punishment." Unfolding his long legs, he settled back against a rock, crossing his arms behind his head. "You must have done something terrible to earn the fate of an outcast."

"I did nothing." Marya whirled around so that her back was toward him. Everything within warned her to hold her tongue, to flee if necessary and leave this dangerous, inquisitive soul behind. But the loneliness of the past year hung around her like a cloud. Even if it was a trap, at least he was speaking to her.

"I am punished for the crimes of my parents. They were fools and believed in fairy tales." The words awakened the ache yet again and brought the familiar lump to her throat. "They refused to bow to the Serpent's rule, trusting in the ancient promises of a mythical King to save them."

She laughed bitterly at the thought and then swallowed as tears threatened to spill over. "The Tribunal handed them over to the Serpent. They died and I was banished for their folly. It is the law of the village, the law of the Serpent." She fixed her gaze on the rocks beneath her feet, not wanting to see him leave. But he *must*—the law required it.

"It is not the King's law. It's not right."

Marya's head jolted up. The stranger had not moved. He sat, still propped against the rock, gaze traveling over the Island from the hills of shattered black rock to the twisted plants and straggling bushes to the gray-shrouded sky above. In his eyes, a strange look smoldered. A mixture of sorrow, anger, determination, and something else—something Marya could not quite name—something almost *tender*.

He stirred, as though he could feel her eyes resting upon him, and turned to face her again. "I am sorry for your loss."

Marya forced a deep breath into her lungs. "They were deluded by false hope. There is no *real* hope on this island."

"You do not share your parents' beliefs then."

It seemed more of a statement than a question. "No, I do not. I cannot. The King is a myth, a shadow from legend. This Island is real. The Serpent is real. I have seen him many times. I have heard his voice and felt the heat of his flames."

The stranger bent toward her, eyes smiling. "What would you say..." His voice grew quiet, like the first whisper of dawn before the sunrise. Marya's breath quickened and she could not help leaning in to hear. "What would you say if I told you that I have *seen* the King and heard his voice? That I have spoken to him as you and I speak now, that I have touched his hand and know him to be real and true. He is no mere legend, Marya, no far-off, forgotten fairy tale. He is alive and ruling today."

Marya set her teeth. "I would have to say that you are lying. There is no other explanation." She flung her hands down at her sides. "Why do you ask me all these questions? I told you what I am. You know the penalty for consorting with an exile, and you must know that anyone who speaks of any king beside the Serpent is condemned already."

"I do."

For a moment, words escaped her. He seemed so calm, so at ease—completely unperturbed by either her outburst or the knowledge of the crime he had committed. "Then… then why do you say such things? Do you wish to die?"

The stranger laughed, a clear golden laugh that brightened the smoggy day. "No man *wishes* to die." He lifted a curved walking stick from where it had lain hidden beside his feet and stood, adjusted the bundle on his back, and strode away in the direction of the village. "Farewell, Marya. I will see you soon."

She remained standing, watching until he disappeared from view over the crest of the hill. Just before passing out of sight, he turned and waved. She hesitated and then started to lift her hand, but he was already gone, and she… she was alone again.

The timbre of his voice struck a pleasant note in her ears—*kindly*, that's what it was. It had been over a year since anyone had spoken so to her. She sank to the ground and tilted her head back to stare at the sky.

If only she could hear Father's voice again.

If she could but catch a glimpse of Mother.

Emptiness overwhelmed her—the emptiness of the ruined hut on the barren hillside, the emptiness she felt inside. Tears, forced back and carried pent up inside during the many long nights of the past year, streamed down, tingling her chapped cheeks.

At length, the flow ceased and she awoke to the world around her again. She breathed deeply and shivered as the cold air flooded her lungs.

Her thoughts seemed as muddled as the thick fog blanketing the island. Who was the stranger? Here in this place of darkness and death, he alone did not seem afraid. In a world of despair, he alone seemed to possess hope. He spoke of the King, even claimed to have seen him, heedlessly breaking the Serpent's law in broad daylight where any listening ear could hear.

He must be mad. Surely that was the only explanation. Only a madman would behave so carelessly.

But how did he know her name?

*****

Snow, again. Marya groaned and shivered beneath her shawl. Three mornings of snow and once more she had awakened to find her fire extinguished and the world covered in a sparkling sea of windswept white. Gusts of icy wind blew the cold powder into her shelter, soaking her to the bone. She curled into an even tighter ball, alternately rubbing her hands and feet to keep them from freezing.

In past years, Marya recalled one, maybe two snowfalls in the middle of winter, but never so many so early in the season. A whirlwind of doubts swirled through her mind, but one troubling matter rose repeatedly to the forefront: how could she possibly manage to survive if this weather continued?

Finding sleep impossible, she crawled out into the formless gray of the snow-clad island. She stamped her feet to restore circulation to her numb toes and winced at the burning and tingling of her skin. Dampness seeped through the thin leather of her shoes.

Overcome with weariness, she slumped on a rock to await the rising sun. The soft whisper of falling snow filled her ears, and she lifted her eyes to the predawn sky. Pristine snowflakes spiraled from the darkness above, as if the stars she occasionally glimpsed through the mist were slowly drifting to earth. For a moment, she forgot to breathe, awed into silence by the sight of such beauty, so rare on the accursed island.

A smile came to her lips and she breathed a sigh of wonder.

As the cold wet bled through her skirt, her attention was drawn back to the frozen earth. Here, on this ragged patch of ground, her father had toiled year after year to grow food for his family. Dead earth spoiled by fire and drought, now hard as rock, offered no hope for survival, and nothing edible remained to be scavenged from the wild.

Marya cursed the snow. No longer would farmers venture beyond the village to work in the frozen fields. No longer would forgetful workmen or flustered housewives leave food lying where quick hands could access it. Those living in the outlying areas surrounding the village would remain hidden in their houses, hibernating until the snowstorms passed.

Driven to rise by the cold, Marya wandered aimlessly over the hill. She found it hard to walk. Her feet had gone numb save for a general burning sensation that deepened whenever she plunged into snow over her ankles. Hunger gnawed at her stomach; it had already been two days since her last meal. If she wanted to survive, she would have to go farther afield and face greater peril than mere wolves.

But the constant cold made even the possibility of facing the Tribunal welcome if it meant an end to her misery.

She realized then that her mind had been made up even as she left the ruins behind, that her feet had followed her unconscious decision and were already steering her toward the one place where she had vowed never to return.

The village.

Somehow the realization gave her strength. She walked faster, exertion granting warmth and energy to her freeing limbs, and finally halted behind the rocky outcrop where she had pilfered the farmer's lunch only a month before. Concealed from prying eyes, she planned her approach to the village and then set off.

A steep climb, resulting in a bleeding knee and aching wrist, brought her to the top of the plateau. The village slowly stirred awake as she crept up and crouched behind an empty barrel, searching for a better place to hide until the villagers filled the streets and she could blend into the crowd. Smoke hovered over sleepy chimneys, and snowcapped doorways gradually yawned open, releasing half-asleep villagers to begin the day's work.

Across the square, Marya spied a wheelbarrow propped against the wall of a bakery. It should provide decent protection from unfriendly eyes until she figured out what *exactly* she planned to do, now that she had arrived. She wrapped Ayanna's tattered shawl over her head and hurried toward the wheelbarrow, taking great care as she skirted the few villagers already in the street. They paid her no mind, hastening along with heads tucked and arms wrapped to their sides to keep in the warmth.

She ducked under the wheelbarrow and curled into the smallest possible ball. A sigh of contentment escaped her lips. Though occasional gusts of wind whipped between the wheelbarrow and the wall, she was free of the falling snow and endless gnawing damp. Heat from the baker's fire seeped through the wall and into her aching bones. Her frozen fingers tingled as she rubbed them together and settled back to watch the day begin in the village.

No dazzling sunrise broke through the fog, but the drab wintry light grew steadily brighter. With the advent of morning, roosters broke into a dissonant symphony, crowing from every rooftop and doorway. The village sprang to life.

Marya gawked at the sheer number of villagers milling about. For so long she had dwelt alone that she found it hard to imagine working and living among so many others.

An old man pushed a cart loaded with kindling past her hiding place, and Marya suppressed a cry. He had been a friend of her father, though she searched her memory in vain to recall his name. It seemed so long ago that he and Father had sat by the fireside and talked for hours on end. She remembered squirming as a child as they carried on boring conversations about King and Kingdom.

She bit her lip at the thought. The sight of her father's friend rubbed raw the year-old wound, and she pressed a hand to her chest in a futile attempt to ease the ache. It seemed unfair that *he* yet lived when her parents were dead and she was an outcast. He had encouraged her father in following the King. *He* was to blame for her father's death—

he and all the others like him who clung to false hopes and kept the legends alive.

The old man staggered through the crowd, cart wobbling and tilting first one way and then the other, threatening to spill at every rut in the street. No one offered help. He pressed on, halting at times to clutch a trembling hand to his back, until he disappeared around a corner.

In his place, a black-robed figure caught Marya's eyes and immediately every muscle tensed. Another one of the Tribunal approached from the opposite direction, and the two halted in front of her hiding place, backs toward her, heads together in whispered conversation.

Maya jerked away from the wall and crouched within the well of the wheelbarrow, stifling her gasping breaths with both hands. Seeing the trailing robes and haunting masks up close carried her back to the Stone. She could almost hear the drums pounding, but then she realized the cadence was the frightful thudding of her own heart. Shielded from the cold, she had grown comfortable—too comfortable. If only for a moment, she had forgotten the Tribunal, forgotten that she was an outcast and that any villager who saw her could turn her in.

The fears which had seemed trivial in her distant shelter now had faces and appeared giant-sized. And yet, the black robes and white masks were less frightening in morning light than in night's shadow. She could almost have dismissed them as ridiculous if she did not know how dangerous the Tribunal priests were.

Finally, the two priests moved on, villagers scattering before them like leaves before a windstorm. Marya realized then what was missing in the village life. Amidst all the bustling and business of the market morning, no smiles brightened the pallid sky, no laughter lightened the mournful sighing of the wind. Sorrow hung over the village like a pall.

Surely it had always been that way, so why did it seem so odd to her now? Words that she had heard a month before repeated in her ears, *"It is not the King's law. It is not right."* Perhaps she would never have noticed if she had not met the stranger. He spoke with such surety, such confidence. *It is not right.*

But who decided what was right, if not the Serpent?

The stranger seemed so utterly different from anyone she saw in the village. His laugh still rang in her ears—a free, joyful sound that, for some reason, made her wonder if the old stories might be more than just fairy tales after all.

Her stomach grumbled and she jumped at the sound, so loud within the confines of her hiding place. The tantalizing aroma of fresh-baked bread wafted around the corner of the bakery against which the wheelbarrow rested. Customers filled the covered porch of the bakery, clutching money bags and fidgeting in line. A cluster of ragged children grouped in front of the open window, eyeing the round loaves of bread the baker set out for customer inspection. Stick-thin arms hugged close to their bodies, legs stamping, the children jogged in place to keep warm.

Marya's mouth watered, and she struggled unsuccessfully to still her shaking hands. The thought of all that food only a few feet away, yet as far beyond reach as if it were buried at the bottom of the Loch, was pure torment. She turned from the bakery and looked across the street where venders hawked their wares. But try as she might to focus on something else, her mind constantly wandered back to the brown loaves the baker had set in his window.

In vain, she reminded herself that she was an outcast. If she were caught—it didn't bear thinking about. Memories from her first trip to the village invaded her thoughts, and she pushed them aside with hunger-fueled bravado.

She wouldn't be caught. Not if she wished to survive.

And she had ventured too far, faced too much peril, to be turned back now at the chance of a little risk.

Determined at last, Marya peered around the side of the wheelbarrow. Market-goers and sellers packed the square. It was now or never. Before she could change her mind, she darted from her hiding place and slipped into the crowd. Ducking elbows and dodging arms laden with purchases, she maneuvered to the far side of the bakery and halted just beyond the window in the shadow of the sign.

The baker stood in the rear of his shop, his back to the open window as he pulled steaming loaves from the oven. For the moment, the bread on the front counter was unguarded. Marya tugged the shawl further over her face. The noise of the crowd jostling past her faded away, and the sound of her own breathing seemed magnified tenfold in the heavy silence.

She gritted her teeth, refusing to retreat though her hands and legs shook with fear, and walked by the bakery as casually as she could. As she passed the window, she shot out her right hand and snatched a loaf of bread, slipping it beneath the cover of her shawl.

It was still hot. The soothing warmth seeped into her hand and spread up her arm. She could almost taste the bread and feel it slipping down her throat, warm and smooth and satisfying.

No one had noticed. Marya slipped back a few paces and then passed by the window again, looking neither to the left or right. A quick movement, so fast even she hardly saw it, and a second loaf vanished into her shawl.

"Hoi! Thief!"

Her heart flew into her throat at the angry shout. The voice sounded familiar. The crowd shifted to her right and she caught a glimpse of the farmer she had robbed a month earlier, flanked by his two sons, waving his arms and pointing at her.

Marya ducked and turned into the crowd.

A second bellow sounded behind her. "I've been robbed!"

The baker—how had he discovered the theft so quickly? She fought the urge to look back. Perhaps if she simply kept walking and stayed away from the farmer, she would not be noticed. Her hopes melted as another cry rang out.

"There's the thief. The outcast girl!"

"Aye, that's her. She robbed me, she did. After her!"

Her nerves failed and she bolted. Still clutching the loaves, one in each hand, she tore through the crowded square. Angry shouts and screams swelled around her as she pushed through, clawing past those who stood in the way. Dimly, as though in a dream, she heard repeated shouts of "Thief!" traveling from person to person, and she groaned— the alarm was spreading.

Grasping hands reached out from every side, tearing at her arms and legs, ripping her shawl from her shoulders. Tugging and kicking, half-sobbing in terror, Marya at last managed to break out of the melee and took off running at full speed back through the village toward home.

She leapt over carts and barrels blocking her path and brushed past surprised villagers with arms full of market goods. Their indignant cries spurred her onward and marked the trail for her pursuers. Pounding feet thundered behind, and rising shouts continued to spread the alert. Marya tucked the loaves beneath one arm and clutched at a stitch in her side.

Risking a glance behind, she felt renewed vigor in her failing legs. It seemed the entire village chased her, faces red with anger, fists raised, many carrying farm implements or other tools as weapons. Several of the Tribunal joined the hunt as well, their black robes flapping, hideous masks grinning insanely as they bore down upon her.

Sheer terror drove Marya past the end of the village, down the steep side of the plateau, across the field and up the opposite slope. Her legs ached with the strain of running uphill through patches of slushy snow. Her lungs burned for air. But there was no hope of stopping yet.

She toiled on, labored step after labored step, until it seemed that the pursuit no longer gained. Something struck the tip of her shoulder as it whistled past, then landed with a clatter on the ground. A rock. She glanced back and saw that several villagers had paused to pick up fist-sized stones and now heaved them at her as they ran. A few of the stones came close, but most fell short as her lead lengthened.

It was a familiar pattern. First the villagers chased, then they threw stones. Eventually, they would stagger to a halt, clutching their knees and heaving for breath, and then throw up their hands in defeat. The outcast had outrun them again.

Gasping and staggering herself, Marya allowed a smile to slip past her lips. Speed and stamina were among the *few* advantages that her life as an exile gave her over the villagers. Soon she would be safe in her shelter with food to eat at last.

Her foot caught on a loose rock and she pitched forward. A jolt of pain snapped through her ankle, and she clutched at it in a panic as the throbbing shot up into her leg. She struggled to her knees and attempted to rise. A cry burst from her lips. Her ankle failed, throwing her down again.

A triumphant shout erupted behind and she knew the villagers had seen her fall. There was no chance they would give up now. Locking her teeth to suppress a groan, Marya forced herself up and set off at a limping run.

A rock struck her in the back, a dull pain between her shoulder blades, nearly knocking the wind from her lungs. A second stone bounced off a rock directly in front of her. It split into tiny flying pieces, and a shard sliced across her leg.

Marya closed her eyes, resisting the despair that dragged at her tired limbs and sought to pull her back. The villagers were close now. She could hear their footsteps just behind and feel their ragged breathing growing closer every second.

Someone grabbed her by the shoulders from behind and threw her down. Stars burst across her vision, and she curled up as tightly as she could to protect herself from the shower of blows to come.

But the blows never fell.

The curses and shouted threats raining down around her were silenced by a single word. "Enough." Though spoken quietly, it was said in such a commanding voice that the mob fell silent as if thunderstruck.

Trembling from fear and pain, Marya peered over the arm she had raised to guard her head. A lone man stood between her and the crowd of furious villagers. He leaned on a walking stick, and a long rectangular bundle hung diagonally from his shoulders.

The stranger.

Face livid with wrath and flushed with the heat of the chase, the baker pushed to the front of the crowd and halted, toe to toe with the stranger, staring him in the eyes. "And who are you to step in the way of justice?" he demanded, a belligerent thrust to his craggy jaw. "The girl is a thief and an outcast. She deserves to be punished. And if you won't step out o' the way, I'll see that you're punished alongside her." He raised knotted fists.

The stranger said nothing but met the baker's challenging glare. For a moment, they stood facing each other, then the baker's red face turned redder still and he backed up a step. The stranger spoke, still in the same unhurried tone, but his every word rang with authority. "Go back to the village. Leave the girl in peace. I will pay what she owes." He opened a small pouch at his belt and removed something that flashed gold in the hand that he offered the baker.

The baker snatched it and held it to his narrowed eye for inspection. Marya could not see what it was, but the baker's mouth fell open and he clutched his closed fist to his floured apron. A look of respect flickered across his face, speedily morphing into one of suspicion.

"Who are you?"

The stranger smiled and spread his arms. "I am a stranger here, as you can see."

"There are no strangers on the Island." The baker eyed him, cocking his head to one side in a way that was almost comical. "Where are you from?"

"A faraway place. That is all you need to know. You would not believe me if I told you more." The stranger turned to leave but the baker forestalled him, barring his path with a log-like arm.

"Like as not. I've heard a lot of tall tales over the years," the baker growled. "This here is the only village on the Island. If you didn't come from here, then you must be an outcast like the girl."

An angry mutter ran through the crowd.

The stranger smiled. "But I am not from the Island."

"There is nothing besides the Island," one of the farmer's sons shouted. "The Island is all there is!"

"I am from the Kingdom."

A gasp spread through the crowd, and Marya picked herself up, wobbling on one foot. Fear for the stranger mingled with fear for her own safety. He *must* be mad to speak so openly about what was forbidden. She examined the crowd, gauging their response. Open disbelief showed on nearly every face—disbelief, wariness, and anger.

"The Kingdom?" The baker retreated, eyes wide with fear. Hostility replaced the suspicion on his face.

The stranger nodded. "The time has come for the promise to be fulfilled."

This was too much. Marya scoffed at the idea. He had rescued her—twice now—and for that she was grateful, but to believe that he was the fulfillment of some ancient legendary promise bordered on the ridiculous. Fearful of joining the crowd that only a few moments ago had been trying to kill her, and yet not wishing to be identified with a madman, Marya limped to the side between the two parties.

"Tales of the promise are fit only for fools or traitors," a deep voice spoke from the crowd, and a tall member of the Tribunal emerged to face the stranger, fingers tightening around the haft of an enormous knotted club. "I am Bjorn," he said, squaring broad shoulders beneath the shapeless black robe, "son of Maddrel, High Priest of the Serpent. The Serpent alone is king. It is forbidden by law to speak of any other. The Serpent alone rules. The Serpent is all there is." His words drifted on the air, a visible challenge.

"The Serpent is a deceiver and a liar," the stranger said, seemingly oblivious to the threatening cloud brewing over the villagers at his words. "Over a thousand years ago, he convinced the villagers to disobey the King and brought them here, to this Island. By their disobedience, the villagers were cursed and bound to the Island, doomed to endure the rule of the Serpent for a time, but not lost forever. The King promised that one day the curse would be broken and the Serpent defeated. That day is now here."

A growl of fury ripped from Bjorn's throat. The crowd took up the furious shout and pressed forward to attack the stranger.

Fear gripped Marya. Surely he would flee now before it was too late, and what would become of her when he did? Robbed of the object of their hate, the crowd would return to their original purpose, and she could no longer run.

But the stranger stood firm as the crowd rushed toward him, screaming for blood, fists held high and weapons brandished. He held up his hand. "Be still."

The crowd halted. Not the ragged halt of a mob lacking leadership or purpose, but an instantaneous stop as if his words had frozen them in their tracks. Speechless and confused, they turned to Bjorn. The Tribunal priest glared at the stranger, hands gripping his club until his knuckles turned white. His body stiffened as though he were about to attack, but he did not move. The tension drained from his muscles, and his arm fell to his side, defeated.

The stranger studied the villagers for a moment, and those who met his gaze quickly looked away, then he turned and strode off at a steady pace. He did not look back and the villagers made no move to follow.

Marya shifted her weight slightly and gasped at the piercing pain in her ankle. She glanced at the villagers as she gathered her strength to flee, if necessary, though she would not be able to get far. But the villagers took no notice of her. They stood still, exactly as the stranger had left them, gaping after him in mixed attitudes of bewilderment, anger, and hatred.

Bjorn roared something indecipherable and spat on the ground. He flung the knotted club away and it pounded into the side of the hill, then he turned, rammed through the crowd, and stormed toward the village. One by one, the villagers dwindled away, straggling back to their hearths.

Marya sensed the turmoil teeming in their minds; she felt it herself. It seemed that all she had once thought to be real and enduring crumbled at the stranger's words and blew away like sand on the wind. Still, a quiet voice whispered doubt in the back of her mind. The Island might be cursed, but it was the only home she had ever known. Though the Serpent was cruel—even evil—he was familiar, not some distant, unknowable legend from the dust of the past.

Yet the stranger's actions compelled her to believe him. He stood face to face with one of the leaders of the Tribunal and was not afraid. He openly pronounced the King and his Kingdom, denounced the Serpent as a liar, and walked away free.

Not even Bjorn, son of the high priest, had been able to stop him.

It made no sense, unless he spoke the truth.

Was it possible that there was something more than the Serpent, more than the accursed Island, more than the death that hung over the villagers every waking moment of every day? Her parents believed there was—and they had paid for their belief with their lives.

If it was true and the King lived, then why had he waited so long to fulfill his promise?

With numb fingers, Marya rubbed her aching head. She knew what she must do. She had to find the stranger and learn the answers to her questions. As she turned to leave, she saw the stolen bread lying where it had fallen when she tripped. Ground almost to mush and covered in layers of grime, it looked far less appetizing than it had sitting in the baker's window. But it was food, and she must survive.

The world turned fuzzy and seemed to tilt as Marya reached for the bread. She blinked, forcing back the blackness encroaching on her vision, and ravenously tore into the loaf of bread. In just a few wolfish bites, she had devoured the entire loaf. The food hit her stomach like a rock, but she searched her hand for the last specks of crumbs. The bread would be gone all too soon, and she would be entirely without recourse. Steeling her resolve, she tucked the second loaf away for a later meal.

Bitter thoughts besieged her as she limped home. She was exhausted and bruised, had injured her ankle and had lost her shawl—a loss she already rued and knew she would rue still more if there were many more snowfalls before the end of winter. Worse still, she had destroyed any hope she had ever fostered that one day she might earn her way back into the villagers' good graces.

It had ever been a vain hope, but a vain hope was better than none at all.

As the shadows lengthened to mid-afternoon and the homeward trip stretched before her, Marya vowed never to enter the village again. This time, she meant to keep her vow. The village was closed to her forever.

*****

Marya paused to scan her surroundings as she crested the last hill, and the slope down to the hut opened before her. Something felt wrong. Tilting her head back, she sniffed the air. There was the faintest trace of a strange scent in the wind. The hair on her arms rose, irritated by the weight of an unknown gaze resting upon her. No one was in sight, but still she could not shake the certainty that she was *not* alone.

Taking great care to avoid loose rocks, she hobbled down the hill. A mere hundred yards separated her from home when she caught a whiff of something burning. Acrid smoke hung on the air and stung her nose.

Someone was down there.

Marya dropped to her knees behind a large boulder protruding from the side of the hill, ignoring the jarring pain that coursed through her ankle at the sudden action. Who was it—villagers... the Tribunal? Had they come to drag her away to the Rahedhenaur, as they had her parents? She rarely kept track of the days, but it must be nearing the Serpent's second coming of the month, though that would not stop a culling from taking place.

A minute passed and still all was quiet. Marya slowly released the stale air from her lungs. No shouts of alarm broke the calm of the late afternoon hour. She must have escaped notice. Now perhaps, she would have a few minutes of respite to decide what to do next.

The villagers must have known where she would go once she escaped, and they must have raced all the way to arrive first. It was a wonder that they had never thought of it before—though perhaps, she had never before angered them enough to warrant the long, wearisome hike.

She glared at the wounded ankle that had slowed her pace. During the long trek, she had felt her ankle swelling inside her tattered shoe. Now, she tentatively fingered the purplish tinted joint. It was hot and prickled at her touch.

Her nose tingled at a new smell, and she tilted her head up to sniff the air. Aside from the pungent smell of a blazing fire, there was something else, another scent that set her stomach rumbling and her mouth to watering: the hearty aroma of meat cooking over flames.

Marya inched to the side of the boulder and peeked around the edge.

A solitary figure, visible from this new angle, stood beside a crackling fire only a short distance from her hut, which was concealed from her view by a stand of boulders. Noting only that the man was not clad in black, Marya glanced at the fire, her gaze drawn to chunks of meat dangling from pointed sticks over the flames. She could almost hear the meat sizzling and feel it melting in her mouth.

The man at the fire stepped across her line of vision as he tended the roasting meat and Marya's heart nearly jumped into her throat. She gulped in a breath of air. Tall, long-legged, light-colored hair—it was the stranger. Casting a last anxious glance around until convinced that it was safe, she finally abandoned her hiding place and limped down toward the fire.

The stranger looked up as she approached, and a smile spread across his face. "I'm glad to see you."

She stammered for a response. "What… what are you doing here?" Up close, the roasting meat smelled even better than it had from a distance. She dragged her attention back to the stranger.

"I wished to speak with you." He knelt beside the fire to tend the skewers. "And you wished to speak with me, did you not?"

"Yes," Marya admitted. Standing here beside the stranger, forced to reckon with his concern for her, brought the deeds of the morning back full force. Her cheeks burned at the thought of the cost of her thievery. She shifted from one foot to the other, winced as her weight rested on her wounded ankle, and finally blurted out, "Thank you for saving me."

He nodded but did not speak, and she found she could bear the silence no longer. She looked away, past him toward the ruins of her hut.

Her mouth dropped open.

The pile of broken rubble that was her old hut was gone. Her shelter had been rebuilt—four walls of unbroken stone, just high enough for her to stand inside if she stooped slightly, crowned with a thatched roof. Wincing at the sharp stab in her ankle, Marya limped inside the shelter, bending her head and shoulders to fit through the low doorway.

A cursory glance revealed that the hut had been furnished with basic necessities: a straw mattress opposite the door, a woolen cloak hanging from a peg, a small stone fireplace set into the wall. Marya rubbed her hands against the cloak, pulled it down and settled it around her shoulders, snuggling into the warm folds of cloth. She bent to examine the wall. Mud filled the chinks between the stones, denying the shrill wind entrance.

How could the stranger have done all of this since rescuing her from the Tribunal? The walk had taken her longer than usual due to her injury, but not that long.

And why would he go to such trouble? Chilled at the possibilities, Marya removed the cloak and draped it over the peg. Retracing her steps until she stood over the stranger, she placed her hands on her hips. "What do you want? Why are you doing this? You know that I have nothing to offer you."

He squinted up at her, confusion wrinkling his brow. "Did I request payment?" She shook her head, and he continued, "Your needs have been met, Marya. They will always be met. There is no longer any reason for you to steal. Do so no more."

Her legs buckled, and she sat before they gave way entirely. "Those stories..." She hesitated, and then swallowing her pride, continued. "They're not just fairy tales, are they?"

"No, Marya. They are not fairy tales."

"Then who are you?"

"I have come to release the villagers." He lifted a skewer and passed it to her. "You know who I am."

"The promised one?" Marya's eyebrows rose as she narrowed her eyes at the stranger, ignoring for the moment the meat in her hands. "And you will free us how? By providing food to the starving and shelter to the cold?"

The stranger laughed. "No, that is just the beginning. There is much more to be done, more than you can now understand." He stared off into the distance toward the shore lying beyond the surrounding hills of rock.

"But the Serpent must be defeated first... innocent blood..." Marya said in a low voice, recalling snippets from her parents' midnight conversations. She looked up at the stranger. "Tell me."

"Tell you what?"

"About the Serpent, about this place, about how all this"—she gestured to indicate the entire Island—"began."

"It's a long story," the stranger warned. He glanced up at the sky and then nodded. "But there is time if you wish to hear it." The rippling flames cast shifting lights across his face and mirrored in his eyes.

"The Serpent is now the King's enemy, but he was once the most trusted knight and loyal servant of the Kingdom. Long ago." A faraway look swept across his face, as though he were wandering the fields of the distant Kingdom rather than sitting beside a sputtering fire beneath the smog of the accursed Island.

Sorrow crept into his voice as he continued his tale. "He was known as Arientyl, chief of the King's knights. For a hundred lifetimes, he served the King faithfully. But then something *changed* within him, and simply serving the King was no longer enough. He desired the King's glory and yearned for the King's power. Driven by his pride, Arientyl attacked the palace, cut down twenty-seven loyal men, and then sought to kill the King in his chambers, still dripping with their blood. But the Prince stood in his way.

"The two battled. For hours they fought, and their combat carried them the length and breadth of the shoreward boundaries of the Kingdom. From the heights of the hills, through the depths of the vineyard, to the green, growing fields."

Marya, listening in rapt attention, thought she heard the distant clanging of metal upon metal echoing down from the long past. Or perhaps it was only the cries of the gulls on the empty shore beyond the hill.

The stranger's eyes, always firm and perceptive, seemed to take on a new aspect as Marya watched, glowing and teeming with knowledge of things yet unknown. "Until at last, on the white sand at the edge of the Loch, both stood their ground. It was fearsome, that final battle. The sand raised by their feet formed a cloud that shielded them from the view of the watchers on the palace walls. So hard did they strike that sparks flew from their blades, the earth shook, and the Loch surged within its boundaries. Yet the Prince had the mastery.

"Arientyl's sword was cast from his hand and the Prince pronounced judgment. For his rebellion, Arientyl was imprisoned in the form of the Serpent and doomed to live forever in the cold vaults of the Loch. Though vanquished, he refused to concede and sought vengeance against the King by enticing the villagers away from their obedience."

"Hadriel," Marya whispered the name with reverence. Her parents had mentioned it time and again in their retellings of the old tales. "My father was descended from her line," she explained. It was something he had considered both a shame—for she had been the first to set foot on the Island—and an honor, for she had also believed first and longest in the King's promise.

"I know." A sad sort of smile flitted across the stranger's face. "Hadriel and the others came to this island hoping to rule as kings. Instead they slaved and perished beneath the iron claw of the Serpent."

Something about the story didn't quite make sense. Marya massaged her forehead and struggled to form the thought into words. "If it is true, then why are there so few who remember? My parents," she explained, "were some of the few villagers who still believe the ancient tales. All the others cling to the worship of the Serpent."

"They cling to death. So few remember because their minds have been poisoned. The gray curtain surrounding the

Island is no ordinary mist. It is the breath of the Serpent. His poison."

Marya shuddered at the thought. "The Serpent's breath?"

"This war is a war of mind and body, Marya." He leaned forward, earnestness pouring from his expression and posture as he explained. "The Serpent lies sheltered in the depths of the Loch, belching forth noxious fumes to encircle the Island. He attacks your minds and your hearts, dulling your understanding. Then he rises to wreak havoc, warring against the body and spreading fear and doubt.

"For a thousand years, the villagers have lived in the mist, dwelling in the Serpent's darkness and daily inhaling his poison, until the memory of the Kingdom has faded from their minds." His voice lowered. "Many claim that the King has forsaken them, but it is the villagers who have forgotten the King."

The fire had burned down to embers, a fascinating display of scintillating shades of crimson and gold. It reminded Marya of the Serpent and the flames that flickered in his iron-bound throat and blazed in his eyes. Like a rush of hot air, the horrible day came back to her as vividly as though she stood again upon the Stone, watching helplessly while the Serpent slew her parents.

She pressed her hands to her temples, trying to erase the heart-rending memories from her mind. "What of my parents, slain for their belief in your Kingdom? What of the King and his promise? If he has not forsaken us, as you claim, then why did he not come sooner?" Her voice trembled. "Why did he not save them?"

For a moment, the stranger said nothing, and doubts coursed to the forefront of Marya's mind. He did not answer because he could not, because there was no answer, just as there was no King.

But at length, he spoke. "Some things are not meant for all to know. Not now, not yet. It is too difficult for you to understand now, but one day, when all things are made new, all will be made clear as well. The time is coming, Marya. It is almost here. The King's plans to rescue the villagers are laid in place and set in stone, and there is nothing the Tribunal or the Serpent can do to hinder them. His promise will be fulfilled."

He spoke with such conviction, such intensity, that Marya felt belief stirring despite herself. Surely he spoke the truth. Never before had she heard words spoken with such weight that her doubts bent before them. At last, she mustered the courage to ask the question she had been longing to ask all afternoon.

"Who *are* you?"

His lips parted in a smile and he started to reply. "I am—" But his words were broken off by an earth-shaking clap of thunder. As the rumbles died away, a change swept over the Island: a difference in the color, the atmosphere, the taste of the air. Cold wind dashed across the hilltops, whistling and wailing as it squeezed through clefts in the rocks.

Dread settled in Marya's stomach. She was on her feet and running before realizing that she had risen. Ankle throbbing, she lurched to the top of the hill overlooking the Loch.

Her heart plummeted.

Dark clouds sped overhead, lightning broiled in the deeps, and the water gathered into a thrashing, roiling, steaming flood. A loud horn call shrilled over the Island, brazen and hope-shattering.

"It is time," Marya said in a breathless whisper. Footsteps halted at her side, and she knew without looking that the stranger had followed her. She lifted her chin, strove to steady her voice, and translated the horn call for his benefit. "He is coming. The Serpent. All the villagers are summoned to assemble in the Rahedhenaur."

"Yes," the stranger said, and she looked up at him. His voice and face were grim. "It is time."

PART FOUR

Light

Death hung on the air. Marya felt it in the bitter wind, tasted it in the mist, and saw it in the eyes of the weeping villagers as they trickled past her, down the rocky path to the shore. Death was coming. A strange, empty calm settled over her—no fear, only indifference. She wiped her clammy hands on her skirt. What did anything matter now? Death took all sooner or later. On leaden feet, she turned and joined the march to the Rahedhenaur.

The mournful crowd gradually swelled, filing into the grim black circle and waiting in silent rows for the arrival of the Serpent. Fear darkened every face. Mothers clasped children to their hearts, fathers whispered farewells to sons and daughters, young wives clung to their husbands' arms, and many hid tear-stained faces in their hands.

Marya had seen it many times before, but the sight was no less heartrending for its familiarity. Nor was the voice that whispered in the back of her mind any less cruel, reminding her that she had no one to stand beside, no hand to hold, no one to mourn for her should she be chosen.

Yet how many of the villagers would find themselves in her position when next the Serpent came? Alone, friendless, forsaken.

She should not wish it on anyone—should not, but a part of her did.

A whisper rippled through the crowd at her approach, and the villagers parted to let her pass, shuffling away as if the brush of a shoulder might infect them with some deadly disease. Even now, in the face of death, she was an outcast. She clenched her fists as she took her place alone, at the far westward side of the assembly.

Soft footsteps approached and halted by her side. She turned to see the stranger standing only a few paces away, staring out over the Loch. Something about him held her gaze. He stood erect—tall, straight, and strong—in complete contrast to the cringing crowd. Not a hint of fear dulled his eyes. Peace radiated from him like heat from a fire on a cold winter's day, and like one kneeling beside a fire, Marya found warmth in his presence.

The gathering storm intensified, wind howling through the ranks of villagers like a pack of wolves. Darkness grew, reaching out to grasp the Island in its deadly hands. With a deep, rumbling roar, the Serpent's head thrust out of the

Loch. Water shot into the air and fell back with a thunderous roar.

Stifled wails broke out among the villagers huddled within the circle of stones as the Serpent's long, armored neck snaked up until he towered over them. Water dripped from his gleaming teeth, fire burned in his eyes, and black smoke exhaled from his nostrils, settling over the Rahedhenaur in a thick cloud.

Poison, the stranger had called it. Marya fought the urge to clasp her hand over her mouth and nose. She shuddered at the sight of the Serpent's deformed hands and forearms—talon-like claws curved at the end of webbed fingers, small in comparison to the rest of his monstrous body, but still horrendously strong. When last she saw her parents, they had been clutched in those claws as the Serpent sank into the Loch.

Death – death – death. The familiar beat of the drums began, heralding the arrival of the Tribunal. The swaying procession of dark robes wove through the crowd, in serpentine fashion to honor their lord, and halted beyond the ring of stones on the brink of the Loch. Maddrel prostrated himself before the Serpent, arms outstretched, forehead touching the sand. The rest of the Tribunal followed suit while Bjorn lifted a sea horn to his lips and blew. As one, the assembled villagers dropped to their knees, heads bowed and hands lifted in silent supplication.

Marya hesitated, legs quivering.

Her head whirled. She thought of her parents standing firm to the death, strong in their beliefs, of the stranger and the certainty of truth that filled her heart when he spoke, of the King and his unfulfilled promise.

The Serpent's head twisted until his baleful gaze rested upon her, and her courage failed. She sank to her knees and bowed her head in submission.

A thousand reproaches welled up inside her, screaming at her, blaming her fear and cowardice. *What have I done?* But even as crushing remorse seized her heart, a second thought arose, dispelling the first like a puff of dust. It didn't matter. Nothing did. For all she knew, the King was a myth and the stranger was deluded like her parents.

Even if the King does exist, what then? We are no better off, still nothing more than a forgotten people on an accursed island, waiting for death to strike.

"We are forsaken." She breathed the words, glancing over at the stranger, who had almost convinced her to believe his lies.

A gasp escaped her lips.

The stranger stood. Alone.

All around him, the villagers knelt in homage to the Serpent, but he stood unafraid. A pang of sorrow gripped Marya's heart, and she clenched a hand to her chest to ease the ache. Did he wish to end like her parents, like all who had gone before them? Cut down in a bloody spray, body reduced to broken splinters, dragged beyond sight and memory beneath the foaming waters of the Loch. Could he not simply kneel and live to see another dawn?

What else was there but each moment of life and then the next, one agonizing breath after another, spent scrabbling on this accursed rock to survive, survive, survive...

What could be worth *dying* for?

Unless the stranger spoke true.

And with that tiny admission of belief, guilt settled upon her like an oppressive weight. The stranger stood, but she had knelt. Conquered by fear, she bowed in worship to the destroyer—clinging to death, as the stranger had said. The thought sent a quiver down her spine, and she endeavored to rise but found that she could not. Strength had deserted her limbs. Terror bound her to her knees like a chain fastening her body to the ground.

Back and forth swung the Serpent's head, slowly scanning the cowering villagers. His gaze swept past the stranger once, twice. Yet, although the stranger stood in direct challenge to the Serpent, refusing to bend knee, he went unnoticed.

Did he not see?

Marya realized that she was holding her breath and slowly exhaled. Bright lights spun before her eyes and her head ached, throbbing with every beat of the drums.

The Serpent's eyes skipped past the stranger once more and his magnetic gaze fixed on Marya. Her tongue clove to the roof of her ash-dry mouth. Time seemed to lengthen in that horrible moment of silence before he spoke. "Come forth, chosen one. It is time."

And Marya obeyed.

She walked forward on unsteady legs, trembling hands clasped to her sides. A black haze invaded her vision, blurring everything save the deep red of the Serpent's eyes drawing her irresistibly nearer. Remembering the steady pace of her father on his way to the Stone, she forced herself to stand tall, marching to her doom.

It is time.

Despairing villagers once more stepped aside as she passed, opening a path to the shore and the Loch and the Stone. She read the relief in their eyes, the loosening of the tension in their shoulders, and felt the release of their pent-up breaths. No doubt they were glad to be rid of her, glad the outcast had been chosen and not one of their own.

Yet who knew how many would be chosen today?

The Serpent waited, mouth agape, eyes shimmering with cruel amusement as she reached the edge of the Loch and began wading out to the Stone. Cold stabbed her legs like dozens of knives. Shivering uncontrollably, she clambered up onto the ice-ringed top of the Stone. Dripping wet, numb with fear, she waited, resisting the urge to drop her eyes to the bloodstained rock beneath her feet.

Images exploded inside her head, like bolts of lightning in a storm. Once again, she saw her parents' motionless bodies lying crumpled on the Stone. Once again, she saw the ruthless triumph in the Serpent's eyes.

Soon it will be my turn.

Though terrifying, the thought struck her as ironic. By kneeling, she had acknowledged the rule of the Serpent and submitted to his authority. Yet the deed had brought her no protection. By kneeling, she had gained nothing and lost everything.

A flash of anger burned within her, consuming her last remaining fears. Anger against the Serpent, anger against the villagers, and even anger against her parents for deserting her, for caring more for a legendary King than for their own daughter. Deepest of all, a seething anger against the King boiled and then surged to surmount all other feelings. Despite the stranger's assurances, the King had failed to rescue.

Again.

Why would such a King deserve my allegiance?

The Serpent spoke above her head, and Marya blocked her ears against the horrible, chilling sound. Twice the Serpent called a name, and two others—the old man she had seen in the village and a small boy—were forced to leave friends and family behind and join her on the Stone to await death.

Marya clenched her jaw to still her chattering teeth. The cries of the grieving villagers seemed distant and faint behind her. Every second felt as long as an hour, time marked by the water droplets falling from the Serpent's head to splash her upturned face.

Then silence fell over the Rahedhenaur, as the Serpent reared back to strike.

A violent tremor shook her body despite her efforts to hold still. She shut her eyes and bowed her head. It would be over soon—a momentary pang and she would be free.

Free of the Island, the Tribunal, and the Serpent.

"Stop!" The cry burst in on her tumbled thoughts.

Her head whipped up.

It was the stranger. He leapt to the brink of the dark water, slinging the bundle from his back and undoing the fastenings with quick fingers. The discarded wrappings fell to the ground, revealing a sword that shone in his grasp, bright and straight and true.

The Serpent halted mid-strike, transfixed at the sight of the rash intruder on his shore. Recognition, horror, and hatred flashed across the monster's face in rapid succession. "You?" The breath hissed between his teeth, and a menacing light filled his eyes.

"Yes, it is I," the stranger said. "I have come." He stepped into the Loch and the water seemed to recede before him, drawing within itself to provide him clear passage.

Marya allowed a cautious breath to fill her lungs when the Serpent's gaze remained fixed on the approaching stranger. He seemed to have forgotten her and the other condemned villagers—the old man and the boy. Whatever happened next, she was still alive, and that was *something* to be grateful for in a life that had offered little reason for thankfulness. A reprieve, however short, was yet another moment to live, to breathe… to hope.

The stranger leapt up onto the stone, and Marya and the others shrank back, yielding a path. He strode to the edge and faced the Serpent, sword raised so the gleaming tip hovered only inches from the beast's nostrils. Orange flames, reflected from the Serpent's gaping mouth, danced across the bright blade.

"I have come," the stranger repeated.

"*Why* have you come?" Hatred blazed in the Serpent's eyes, hatred so intense that Marya could not keep from trembling with fear. "They chose *me*. A thousand years ago, you were rejected, ignored, forgotten. Now, they do not even recall your name."

"I have come to remind them. To take back what is mine and reclaim my people. You will not harm them any longer."

Light gathered around the stranger, a light that radiated from within, in stark contrast to the billowing blackness that emanated from the Serpent and hung over the entire Island.

"The sword cannot rescue them. You know the law. Blood must pay the price of wrongdoing." The Serpent hissed and there was laughter on his breath—savage, harsh, clacking laughter, but Marya thought she detected a faint trace of something else as well.

Was it... *fear*?

The stranger hefted the shimmering sword in his hand. "The price will be paid." Instead of striking, he spun and flung the sword away. It whirred, thrumming through the air, before knifing down and sinking into the Loch.

Instantly, the waves fell silent and the wind died.

The stranger turned back to the Serpent, facing him with arms spread wide. "I have come. You will take me." There was no questioning the authority in his voice. It was not a suggestion, nor an offer. It was a command.

Thunderstruck, the Serpent fell silent, then his jaws opened in a wide, ghastly grin. "Yes, I will take you, O Son of my Enemy."

The Serpent struck.

Marya's horrified scream caught in her throat and lodged fast. Gasping, she closed her eyes and buried her head in her hands, unable to watch. Muted sounds fell on her ears—a muffled groan of agony from the stranger, a hiss of pleasure from the Serpent, the clack of his jaws, and a wet thud as he released the body.

A long moment of silence passed before Marya raised her head, peering through her knotted hair. A gruesome sight met her eyes. The stranger sprawled across the Stone in a crumbled heap. He had fallen on his side so that his face was hidden from her, though his body was so torn and covered in blood that she could scarcely tell how he lay.

The Serpent's savage face hovered over the body, a brief tongue of flame spurting from his bloodied mouth with every ragged breath he took. Rearing his monstrous head to the sky, he raised a triumphant, reverberating roar to the swirling dark clouds above. The sound engulfed the Island, bouncing back from every crevice, crack, and split in the rocks. Widening ripples spread across the water, the Stone shook, and blackness spun over Marya's vision.

Then the Serpent's head flashed down again. Grasping the stranger's body in his skeletal jaws, he whirled around, plunged into the water, and was gone.

*****

Tears sprang unbidden to Marya's eyes and she, so accustomed to the sight of death, could not say why. She was alive. The Serpent had forgotten her in his triumph over the stranger's death. She should be relieved.

The stranger had received only what all fools deserved. What had he hoped to accomplish by challenging the Serpent? To rescue the villagers by offering himself in their stead? A vain hope. The Serpent would return—if not today, then tomorrow, or a few days hence. The Rahedhenaur would continue, and the villagers would suffer for the stranger's foolishness.

The Serpent would feast on their blood until the Island crumbled before the steady onslaught of time or until the villagers had all succumbed to his insatiable appetite.

She looked back down at the Stone. Dark blood, still wet, pooled in the crevices where the stranger had lain. The pool spread, creeping across the rock until the entire flat top was covered in the crimson tide. She jumped back, but there was no way to escape it. The stream coursed over her feet and slowly seeped into the rock, turning the Stone a deep red. Then... gradually... the color faded until it vanished, taking with it the stains of all the deaths of the past. The Stone gleamed pure black in the ashen gloom.

"Who was that man?" A breathless voice spoke beside Marya's ear, and she started at the sound. She had almost forgotten about the others who had been chosen with her—the old man and the boy. It was the old man who had spoken, and at the cracking of his voice—a voice she had often heard arguing about the Kingdom with her father—his name at last sprang unbidden to her mind: Taban.

She shrugged in response to his question. "A stranger. A fool. I know not."

"The Serpent called him the son of his enemy," Taban persisted, pale blue eyes watering. "If the ancient tales speak true, then that would make him..." His quavering voice trailed off into nothingness.

The weight of his unspoken words settled on Marya. "But... that is impossible."

"Impossible, perhaps. Incomprehensible, doubtless. To be sure, I cannot understand it." He shook his hoary head and reached out a trembling hand to touch her shoulder. "But it was said that long ago the King promised to send a rescuer."

Marya pulled away from his touch. "And just how do you suppose we will be rescued by a dead man?" The bitterness of her words clung to her tongue, and she swallowed before speaking again. "There is no rescuer, no Prince, no King, no ancient promises. There is only the Serpent."

There is only death.

The sooner everyone acknowledged the truth, the better.

Taban pursed his lips and seemed about to disagree with her, but his words were cut off by a crack of lightning overhead. For a second, the entire sky lit up in a ghostly glow. Thunder rumbled in the deeps. The earth trembled. Instinctively, Marya dropped to her knees, clinging to the rough surface of the Stone.

Shrieking wind tore across the Island, discharging a flurry of hailstones that shattered on the rocks. The wind lashed the water into enormous waves that dashed against the shore, shooting flecks of foam high into the air. Dark clouds brewed overhead and then burst, releasing a torrent of rain upon the forlorn villagers still huddled in the circle.

A blood-chilling scream rose from the depths of the Loch and sped toward the Island, eclipsing all other sounds. It resounded from the crescent hills, until it seemed that the very rocks screamed in pain. Then the cry shriveled into a death rattle and faded away.

Utter darkness fell.

Waves crashed over Marya's head and nearly tore her from the Stone as they fell back again. She scrabbled for a better handhold, hanging half on the Stone and half in the roiling water. Sheets of rain hammered down, stinging beads of frozen water pelting her arms. Her muscles spasmed and she struggled to maintain her grip, fighting the terror rising in her throat at the appalling might of the storm.

At last, its wrath appeased, the storm stilled. The waves faltered and fell back, the Island became steady once more, while the rain slackened to a misty drizzle and then drifted away.

Marya struggled to the top of the Stone and lay on her back, panting for breath.

A few moments ago, the water separating the Stone from the Island had been a tumultuous sea. Now the Loch appeared as tranquil as the dawn. Her gaze traveled to the shore where bedraggled individuals slowly separated from the clusters of villagers and resumed their places in the Rahedhenaur.

Marya stood and helped her companions rise. The boy clutched at her hand, tears trickling down his cheeks. She drew back, skin prickling at his touch, then wrapped her free arm around his shoulders and gave a reassuring squeeze. She spoke to Taban over the boy's head. "What do we do? Leave before the Serpent returns?"

Hope gleamed through the tears in the boy's eyes and he nodded his head. But Taban did not answer. His eyes fixed unblinking on the Loch, he stood still, as if frozen in place. Then he sighed and closed his eyes, bowing his white head.

"Taban." Marya placed a timid hand on his shoulder, noting how thin and frail he was beneath his ragged clothes. "Let us leave."

"No." His voice was as strong and unyielding as iron, but he did not shy from her touch—from the touch of an outcast. "No, we must wait."

"For what?" She tossed her head back and fixed as fierce a glare as she could muster. "For the Serpent to return?"

The boy tugged at her hand. "Please, let's just leave."

"No, we must wait. Simply wait." Taban relaxed slightly and the edge faded from his tone as he hugged the boy to his side. Marya pulled her hand from the boy's grasp and retreated a step from the crazed old man. "I know not why, my children, but I feel that something is going to happen, something marvelous, and we must wait to behold it!"

Would she be surrounded by fools all her life?

She glanced back at the shore—so near and yet too far. The Tribunal had regained their feet and now clustered at the water's edge, soaked black robes draping their frames as the mist cloaked the Island. There was no chance for an escape now. She would not be able to get far before feeling the point of a spear in her back.

Resigning herself to her fate, Marya turned to face the Loch and at once caught her breath. Something was missing. The air seemed so still, free from the perpetual wailing of the harsh wind. Instead of the familiar bite of frigid air, Marya felt a warm breeze dance across her face, bearing with it the scent of life, freshness, and of clean, growing things. A strange feeling of expectancy stirred within and hovered around her. It was almost as if she and all the others *were* waiting, just as the old man had said.

Waiting for something to happen, though she did not know what.

Taban tensed, straightening up so unexpectedly that he nearly overthrew the boy. "What is that?" He craned his neck to stare across the Loch, a puzzled expression wrinkling his weather-beaten face.

With trembling hands, Marya brushed her dripping hair out of her eyes. "What do you see?" A twinge of fear thrummed in her chest, despite her efforts to quell it. "Is it the Serpent?"

"No, no. Not the Serpent. Tell me what you see *there.*" He raised a crooked finger and sighted along it.

Marya peered toward the spot his finger indicated. There, the Loch gathered into a strange, swirling circle of water. The whirlpool spun faster and faster, the speed and fury of the lashing current thrusting the sides up slightly out of the water. In the middle of the churning maelstrom, a gleaming object caught her gaze, flashing as the water whipped it this way and that, bobbing up and down, now above the waves, now below.

The boy recognized it first. "It's his sword."

Glinting silver and gold, the stranger's sword rose from the water, lifted by the mounting eddy. Then as swiftly as it had begun, the whirlpool died away and the waters resumed their normal course. The sword remained floating on the misty Loch, rocking back and forth on the undulating waves.

"But how can it do that?" the boy asked. "Don't metal things sink in the water?"

Taban gave no reply, his gaze intent on the bobbing blade.

A few yards from the sword, ripples spread over the surface of the water. The Loch shuddered and quivered in widening rings.

Marya's breath came fast and furious as she watched. She could no longer deny that the old man had been right. Something was about to happen. An odd tension hung over the Island, like the heavy moment of silence before the first stroke of a storm. A great quiet, as if all living things had stilled and were watching, waiting to witness an event the likes of which the world had never seen.

The water parted, shattering the rings of ripples, and tumbled away with a concerted roar. A tall figure rose from the midst of the disturbance and stood on the mist-shrouded waves as on solid ground.

Taban gave a hoarse shout of joy. "It's him!" he cried, and his ancient voice no longer sounded feeble. Endowed with new strength, his voice carried to the shore and the farthest side of the Rahedhenaur. "It is the Prince!" Tears spilled from his eyes, running down the grooves of his worn cheeks.

The breath drained from Marya's lungs. She stared at the distant figure, trying to make sense of what she witnessed. Only a short while ago, she had seen the stranger torn and broken, the life fled from his lungs, undoubtedly dead. No man could have survived the Serpent's assault. No man could have lost so much blood and lived.

Yet now he stood on the water, *alive*.

Her knees shook, threatening to give way. "Is it a phantom? A ghost?"

"No," Taban snorted. "Not a ghost. Use your eyes, child. It's the Prince! He is alive!"

Marya pressed her heels against the Stone, taking comfort in the cold, hard reality of the rock beneath her feet. Here at least was something she *knew* to be firm and solid.

Her gaze reverted to the distant man as he threw his head back and laughed. It *was* the stranger. She would recognize that sound anywhere. No longer clad in tattered rags, he wore a gleaming suit of full armor with a white surcoat and a long blue cape that trailed behind him. Tall and strong and whole, he stood upon the water, luminous and victorious.

The stranger reached for the floating sword and it flew into his grasp, ablaze with white flames. Water droplets fell from the blade, reflecting the luster of the sword in a thousand tumbling rainbows. He sheathed the sword and strode across the dark water, over the bottomless depths toward the shore. At his first step, the last waves fled and the Loch became as smooth as glass beneath his feet.

"The Light has come!" Taban cried, voice cracking in his excitement. "The promise has been fulfilled."

Marya shook her head. "I don't understand. He died. I *saw* him die. Just like all the others."

Chuckling, the old man spread his arms wide as if the answer were the most obvious thing in the world. "Innocent blood has done it."

"I don't know what you're talking about."

But the words caught on her stubborn tongue. She did know, didn't she? How many times had she overhead her parents speaking about the Promise and the Light and the innocent blood that must pay the penalty? How many times had she heard… but refused to listen?

Taban took her by the arm and his eyes were filled with gentleness. "You remember, child, from the ancient tales? 'When with innocent blood the price of wrongdoing is paid, Light shall rise from the Darkness, and Darkness shall be slain.' Innocent blood has paid the price." His hand shook as he gestured toward the approaching man. "And the Light has risen."

The full meaning of his claim struck Marya like a blow, and she staggered before it. The stranger who had befriended her, rescued her from the villagers, supplied her needs, and rebuilt her hut, was the Prince. Still the confession lodged in her throat. Acknowledging the stranger as the Prince meant accepting the King and his Kingdom; it meant rejecting the Serpent forever.

There was no longer any hope in denying the truth, since she could no longer reject it as a lie. So many years she had deluded herself, playing the fool while blaming her parents for their foolishness.

She recalled the gathering in the Rahedhenaur and the call to worship the Serpent. Instead of standing as she knew she should have, she had followed her craven heart and knelt—knelt like a coward, knelt like the traitor she was. Could the Prince forgive a traitor's heart?

The Prince reached the Stone, and Marya instantly fell to her knees and bowed her head. Rustling behind told her that Taban and the boy knelt as well. Tears swam in her eyes as she studied the intricate patterns carved into the black rock by centuries of wind and rain.

Then the Prince's boots stepped into her field of vision and halted.

Each second that passed weighed heavier and heavier upon her shoulders, and still the Prince did not speak. Marya bit her lip until she tasted blood on her tongue. He knew of her failure. He had witnessed her denial when he stood near her in the Rahedhenaur. Why then did he not bring accusations? Perhaps he had nothing to say to her, no words—not even of condemnation—to waste upon a traitor.

Finally, when she could no longer bear waiting, Marya raised her head, and the Prince smiled at her. She gasped at the love beaming from his eyes. It washed over her, so bright and fierce that it almost hurt—a cleansing pain. Shame and sorrow overwhelmed her. Tears streamed down the hands she cupped across her face. Rocking back and forth, she sobbed, heart-wrenching cries issuing from her soul.

I denied him. I bowed to the Serpent. I am a traitor.

His mail clinked on the Stone as he knelt beside her and raised her head. Blinking through a haze of tears, Marya saw that he smiled still. "Why do you cry, Marya?" he asked.

The tears gushed out harder and faster than ever, and she could not summon more than a whisper in response. "You know what I have done. Why do you speak kindly to me?"

"Marya, dear child, all is forgiven."

She shook her head. "It cannot be…"

But even as she spoke, she looked into his eyes for the first time and suddenly *knew*—all *had* been forgiven. Why, she knew not. She did not deserve it, but she had been forgiven nonetheless. Peace swept over her, calming the turmoil in her heart.

The Prince extended his hand and lifted her to her feet then turned and did the same for Taban and the boy. Her hand tingled from the strength of his grip. He was no phantom, no mere shade or ghost as she had at first supposed. He was solid and real, and of the many injuries he had suffered, no sign remained save a single white scar that carved across his neck. He seemed majestic now, powerful and strong beyond imagining.

A quiver of fear stirred in Marya's stomach. But the fear the Prince inspired somehow felt entirely different than the fear of the Serpent, though she could not say why. Questions rose in her mind but apprehension silenced her tongue. Confusion and bewilderment broiled within, as fierce and thundering as the storm which had swept across the Loch.

The Prince smiled at her. "What is it you would ask, Marya?"

She hesitated, but his warm smile made her forget her fears. "Sire, why?"

The Prince apparently understood the meaning of her vague question, for he answered without hesitation, "I came to fulfill my Father's promise from long ago. Innocent blood alone could pay the price of the faithless and redeem them. Innocent blood alone could defeat the Serpent and end the reign of death." He paused, allowing the explanation to soak in, then said with a wink, "There is yet one thing to be done."

He turned to the peaceful waters of the Loch. In a voice of absolute command and authority, he called the Serpent by the name he had borne before he fell into shadow. In the long years of darkness, the name had grown so twisted and tainted with evil that the mere utterance now seemed to hang on the air like a foul black cloud.

"Arientyl, come forth!" The Prince's cry rang across the Loch like the blast of a trumpet, a summons that could not be disobeyed.

The Serpent burst from the Loch with a cry of fury. His burning gaze settled on the Prince, and a fearsome look of horror twisted his face, terror visible beneath the hatred blazing in his eyes.

He is afraid.

The thought was startling. Having endured the Serpent's iron rule for so long, Marya found it inconceivable that *he* could fear as well. Yet the reality showed clearly in his heaving breaths and twitching claws.

"Come," the Prince commanded.

The Serpent obeyed. He did not seem able to do otherwise. Drawn against his will, body writhing with the strain, he approached the upright figure of the Prince.

Marya shrank back as the monster swayed to a halt just a few yards from the Stone. Malice and fury blazed so intensely in his eyes that she felt her knees wobbling. She retreated, longing for a place to hide. Then she caught sight of the Prince's face and stopped, her fear melting like snow in the noon heat.

How could she be afraid while standing at the side of the one who had defied death itself? The Prince called and the Serpent came. He commanded and the Serpent obeyed. A thrill ran through her, and she shivered, not from fear or cold, but from anticipation.

The Prince addressed the Serpent, and his countenance was terrifying to behold, so great a power and majesty were revealed in him. Before him, the Serpent cowered and sought to break free, cringing and groaning with each laborious breath, but a word held him fast.

"You have chosen pride and arrogance," the Prince declared. "You have chosen the way of rebellion." He drew his sword from its scabbard with a soft, musical *shiinnnggg*, and metallic humming filled the air. Resplendent in glory, the blade mirrored the light of its wielder and erupted in white flames. It shone like a dazzling star amidst the Serpent's smog. The beast shrieked at the brightness, but he could not escape it.

The Prince tightened his grip on the hilt and stepped down from the Stone. "You have chosen your doom." Lifting the flaming sword in his hand, he charged toward the Serpent.

Baring jagged teeth, the Serpent surged to meet the Prince, his passage painting a white-tipped wake across the Loch. Marya held her breath as the Prince waded farther from the shore and the distance between man and monster dwindled. The Serpent's head dipped to one side, spewing fire into the Loch. Black steam engulfed the combatants as they met with a thunderous clash and a flurry of sparks. The final battle began.

At first Marya could see nothing through the cloud, then the pure white light of the sword pierced the darkness and an answering spurt of flame coiled around it. The steam dissolved, and the Prince appeared.

Circling, moving as lightly over the waves as if he were walking on firm ground, he held his sword at the ready. The Serpent lunged, and he sidestepped, then darted forward with a striking speed that rivaled that of the monster. His sword flashed, triggering a screech from the Serpent. Boiling blood steamed down the beast's back from a wound in his left shoulder.

A stream of flame stabbed at the Prince, and he brought up his blazing sword to shield his face. Before he could recover, the Serpent's spiked tail whipped through the water, smashing into his legs. He fell on his back, rolled as the beast's head descended, and charged. Ducking beneath a claw slash, he leapt onto the Serpent's armored back.

Barely dodging the monster's sweeping teeth, the Prince gripped the serried rows of ridged scales with his left hand while unleashing a blinding barrage of blows with the sword in his right. Though his opponent's scales were hard as iron, the Prince's sword was keen and sharp. The glowing blade sang through the air, drawing blood again and again.

Louder and louder the Serpent shrieked as his efforts to shake off his unwanted rider proved futile and his repeated attempts to blast the Prince to oblivion with fire proved vain. Marya watched the conflict in horrified amazement. Though the Serpent fought with all his might and main, striking savagely with tooth and claw and spewing venomous breath, the Prince proved to be the master.

With the fury of despair, the Serpent wound his coils around the Prince and dragged him into the depths. Down, down they went, struggling, fighting still, till Marya was sure that both must be dead.

The battle suddenly returned to the surface, a blinding chaos of thrashing waves and wild spray. Bright flashed the sword in the strong hand of the Prince; many and serious were the deadly wounds which it inflicted on the Serpent. Yet though the vile monster strove his hardest, not once was he able to injure the Prince. The mighty combat raged until the Loch was lashed with foam and streaked with the blood of the Serpent.

Light battled darkness. Life battled death.

At last, the Prince threw down the Serpent and stood with the point of his sword at the beast's throat. Defiant to the last, the beast glared up at his conqueror. Even in the face of defeat, there was no remorse in his face, no plea for mercy on his forked tongue.

"Do it," he growled. "Slay me and end this. A true warrior would have done so long ago." His form twitched and seemed to dissolve. For a moment, Marya caught a glimpse of the faint outline of a black-clad knight, kneeling on a white beach as breakers surged around him.

His voice seemed to come from a great distance. "Or are you incapable of the deed? Ever has weakness been your downfall."

The knight's hand reached to his boot and he lurched up, a dagger flashing in his hand.

The image faded and she beheld the Serpent again. Even at a distance, she detected a sudden change across his face. Was it the unseen flicker of an eyelid? A twitch of his throat? Somehow, she *knew* he was going to strike.

"Watch out!" she screamed.

The Serpent belched a raging ball of fire and dove into the inferno, carrying the Prince with him. White light exploded within the fireball, scattering and consuming the orange flames. Within moments, the Prince emerged unscathed, standing on the prone body of his enemy. Smoke curled from the tip of his sword.

"Your doom is death," the Prince stated, stepping away from his rival and moving toward the shore.

The flames raging in the Serpent's throat burst forth and wrapped around him. He screeched, writhing and thrashing in the water in a vain attempt to douse the fire. Black smoke vented through the seams in his scales. The fire surged across his body until his iron-plated hide melted in the heat, but his flesh, though burning, remained unconsumed.

The Prince turned to the Loch. "Waters," he called, stretching out his arms and pulling them back in a wide sweeping motion, "arise!"

A tremor shook the surface of the water and ripples shivered to the horizon. Then the Loch split and a cavernous gulf yawned before the Prince's feet. Walls of water rose to towering heights overhead... and then plunged to swallow the Serpent.

There was an audible hiss, and a fountain of steam rocketed into the air when the falling torrent met the raging fire. Limbs flailing, screeches shaking the foundations of the Island, the Serpent was drawn into the gaping mouth and submerged beneath the receding waves.

The swirl of fire drifted steadily deeper and deeper until it disappeared in the unknown depths of the Loch.

The Serpent was gone.

*****

"Gone." Marya whispered the word to herself, blinking in disbelief. It seemed impossible, yet she had witnessed it with her own eyes. The Serpent was gone! She felt somehow lighter, freer, as if a great weight had been removed from her shoulders.

White spray drifted down on the wings of a breeze as the Prince sheathed his sword and strode back toward the Island. "It is done." He beckoned Marya and the others to leave the Stone and follow him as he waded to the shore and halted before the assembled crowd.

Awed silence hung over the Rahedhenaur, and for a long moment, the villagers simply stared at their deliverer, stunned. Then, like a ripple slithering across the Loch, they knelt, one by one bending knee to the one who had defeated the Serpent.

Outright fear clouded many faces, while worry and uncertainty marked others. For a moment, Marya struggled to understand. Did they not realize that they were free from the Serpent and his reign of terror? She looked to Taban, but his gaze was fixed on the Prince; he had no eyes or ears for anything else.

At last, it dawned upon her. No doubt the villagers feared that they had merely exchanged one tyrant for another. The Serpent's reign had ended, but the Prince would take his place. The same cloud of fear and death would continue to rule over them. They would never be free.

The Prince's laughter filled her ears.

Loud, clear, and pure, it swept around and swallowed her. For several moments, no other sound could be heard. The accursed Island itself was as silent as death, as though stupefied at the startling demonstration of joy. But the Prince's laughter was contagious.

Before she knew what had happened, a laugh bubbled up inside of Marya and burst from her lips, merry as the morning sun. The boy caught it next, giggling behind his hands, his tear-stained face smiling and bright. The laughter spread. First, a contained chuckle escaped here and there, then as more joined in, the sound swelled until the whole assembly raised a laugh so full and mighty and overflowing with such thanksgiving that the Island shook to its roots for the second time that day.

When at last the laughter died down, though not the joy that it had brought, the Prince spoke to the villagers. "Death has reigned here too long, but today its power has been crushed." His eyes twinkled and his voice rang out over the Loch in summons. "Waters, let the dead arise!"

The dead... A chill crept over Marya's heart. *What is he doing?*

The Loch shuddered and hundreds of figures surfaced from the water between the Island and the Stone. A gasp burst from the crowd, and Marya swallowed the familiar knot of fear constricting her throat.

The dead stood dripping on the shore.

She cringed, dreading what damage the ages of decay would have wrought upon their bodies. Then, summoning her courage, she gazed upon them. Water coursed from their clothes and hair. They looked strong and hale as they surveyed the world through eyes bright with wonder. Stumbling a little, like toddlers unaccustomed to the strength of their legs, they advanced toward the villagers.

The first moment of surprise past, cries of joy broke out among the villagers as families and friends beheld dear familiar faces, long lost, now restored, and rushed toward them. The two groups intermixed, laughing, joking, and crying.

A tear slipped from Marya's eyes and rolled down her cheek as she watched the happy scene. Then she saw them.

"Mother! Father!" She raced across the rocks and fell into their arms, sobbing and laughing at the same time. Corridan's whiskers brushed her hair as he bent to kiss her forehead. Ayanna clutched her to her chest, arms trembling, as if she would never let go.

Marya tried to speak, but her thoughts refused to form into words. At such a time, words seemed wholly inadequate, incapable of conveying emotion or meaning or depth. Arm in arm, the three slowly walked back toward the gathering in the Rahedhenaur.

A dark-haired young woman was standing at the Prince's side, but she was pulled away into the crowd by laughing children as they approached. The Prince looked up and smiled, grasping Corridan and Ayanna by the hands. "Well done, strong Corridan and faithful Ayanna, true to the death. Your names are held in high honor in my Father's house."

Ayanna laid her gentle hand on the Prince's while her eyes shimmered with unshed tears. "We have long awaited your coming."

"My liege." Corridan bowed, with wonder in his voice. "You have borne much to rescue us from the Serpent."

"It is now finished. The Serpent is destroyed and the curse is ended. It is time to leave." The Prince turned to address the villagers. "Come with me to my Father's house. This Island is accursed, stained by the poison of the Serpent's breath, and will not be suffered to darken the world much longer." His words lingered in the air, a hint of coming doom.

Taban straightened his stooped shoulders and hobbled to the Prince's side. He motioned to the villagers. "Well, what are you waiting for? This place certainly isn't paradise."

Marya laughed and ran to join him, followed by her parents and the boy. Within moments, the gathering around the Prince swelled. Among the throng, still clad in the black robes and white mask of the Tribunal, was Bjorn.

"That's something I never thought I'd see," Corridan muttered.

Bjorn halted in front of the Prince and tore the mask from his face, casting it to the ground. Then he lifted the curved sea horn hanging at his side and stomped it underfoot. It crunched beneath his heavy boot, breaking into jagged pieces, which he resolutely ground into dust. Tears coursed freely down his cheeks as he clenched and unclenched his fists in obvious apprehension.

"Well," he stated gruffly, "I've come."

"Bjorn!" Maddrel materialized from the shadows of the Rahedhenaur, mask clinging to his rage-contorted face. "Traitor! Fool! Will you reject all that you have lived for? Will you reject your people? Your own father?"

Square jaw set like granite, Bjorn stood still and unyielding, the muscles working in his cheeks as he bore his father's wrath.

"Imbecile!" Maddrel shrieked. "You will not answer me? I swear, for your treachery, though you are my son, I myself would slay you here as the Serpent's law demands." He brandished his ornamented staff like a weapon and took a step closer.

"Father." Bjorn held up his hands to forestall Maddrel's attack. His deep, rumbling voice was calm and assured. "The Serpent is gone. Do you not see that we were wrong to serve him and deny the King? Look around you. See the destruction the Serpent has brought upon us."

"Enough." Maddrel's voice cracked like the snap of a whip. "Enough. No son of mine could speak so. You are my son no longer. Be gone with you—you and your traitorous friends!" He spat, and without a backward glance, turned from his son and strode away.

Bjorn took a step after the thin figure limping slowly away from the Rahedhenaur and then stopped, watching until Maddrel disappeared over the top of the hill. The big man bowed his head, sorrow etched in the lines of his face.

The Prince placed a comforting hand on his shoulder. "He made his decision long ago, but that need not rule yours. You have made the right choice."

Gradually the crowd of villagers in the circle of stones dwindled, many making their way to stand beside the Prince. Some came eagerly, joy stamped on their hopeful faces; others came uncertainly, trembling between fear and awe; still others walked forward with an effort, casting sorrowing glances behind. But one by one, all the villagers faced the same choice and made their decision. The few who remained turned and hiked up the long, winding path into the hills, following the footsteps of Maddrel.

"I don't understand," Marya whispered. "Why won't they come?"

Beside her, Taban sighed and bowed his head. "They worshiped the Serpent in the darkness until their minds were destroyed by his lies. They cannot see the mercy of the Prince or trust in his promises, and the Island is all they know. They would rather remain, scorning the Prince's offered grace, than leave the darkness that is familiar to them. Poor souls. Like the Serpent, they have chosen the way of death."

With a heavy heart, Marya turned from the sight of the wretched villagers trailing away from the Rahedhenaur. Her attention refocused when the Prince summoned her to the edge of the Loch.

"Marya, come and see." He pointed towards the distant horizon. Across the shimmering water, a white speck glinted against the dark horizon. It grew as it neared, until Marya could identify the object as something from the legends. "A sail?"

He nodded. "My Father sent his ship to carry all of us home to the Kingdom."

Home. The Kingdom.

A tremor of excitement ran through Marya. What wonderful images those words evoked—things she had only dreamt about or heard mentioned in ancient lore. Soft green fields, sweeping hills, tall trees, azure skies. She gazed at the dark clouds still looming overhead, a constant threat. What would a *blue* sky look like? How would it feel to stand in the sun, its warm rays caressing her cheeks, or to listen to soft breezes sighing through tall grass or stately trees?

The ship approached swiftly, driven by a pleasant wind, then slowed and came to a gentle stop before the Island. Built of gleaming white wood, intricately carved and masterfully crafted, the ship boasted a prow in the figurehead of a dove whose back-stretched wings formed the sides of the vessel. White silk sails billowed from carved spars and shimmered with pure light, yet just by looking at them Marya knew those sails were as strong as iron and able to withstand the fiercest storm. The sighing breeze stroked the taught rigging like a harpist's hand upon the strings, gently caressing the ropes and lines until they sang with a soft strain of music that drifted along with the ship.

Led by their deliverer, the faithful climbed up the gangplank, eager to embark on the magnificent vessel. The Prince grasped the wheel; the white ship came to life beneath his touch and scudded out across the Loch.

Perched in the prow between Corridan and Ayanna, Marya watched the ship slicing through the water, its sharp keel leaving a bubbling white wake. But it could not move far enough or fast enough to suit her.

Unexpectedly, the ship slowed and came to a stop. The sails slackened and hung limp from the spars, unstirred by the wind. Marya started to her feet, a knot of fear in her stomach. Had the Prince changed his mind about rescuing them from the Island? It was still so near—too near for comfort. Did he mean to send them back?

In the stern the Prince rose, silhouetted against the dark, brooding shape of the Island. "It is time!" He leapt onto the transom, gripping a line for balance, and pointed toward the rocky shore. "The time for judgment has come. Witness the mighty hand of the King! The accursed Island shall be no more."

The villagers crowded to his side in the stern of the motionless ship. As the last echoes of his voice died away, a deep rumbling filled the air. Violent tremors shook the Island, and rings of disturbance shot across the water. A moment's stillness, then with a roar, streams of molten lava burst from the crevices of the black rock.

Hissing like a thousand serpents, the torrent of fire spewed across the face of the Island, melting stones in the heat. Shrieking fireballs shot from the cracks. Anguished cries rang out from the remaining villagers as they fled in vain before the rushing tide—desperate cries that carried across the water to the ship.

The Island crumpled, collapsing in on itself in a jumbled roar of falling stones and liquid fire. With a roar, the Loch rose and the accursed rock, along with the villagers who had denied the Prince, sank into the water's embrace and vanished from sight.

Stunned silence hung over the ship and all the villagers on board.

Sorrow marred the Prince's face as he gazed out across the churning waves. "The way was open to them to come, but they chose the way of the Serpent and so now they must share in his doom. Judgment is complete." A light shone in his eyes. He flung his head back, spread his arms to the heavens and cried, "All shall be made new!"

At his command, the dark mist covering the Loch fled, scattering before a warm breeze. Blue sky shone clear overhead, and for the first time in centuries, the villagers were able to behold the light of the sun.

Light.

Marya reveled in the wondrous sight, her unaccustomed eyes watering at the intensity. She took a deep breath and then another, filling her lungs with new, clean air. The foul, choking smell—the Serpent's poison—was gone, and the air was unsoiled and fresh. Below, the muddy blackness slowly faded from the Loch until the water glistened crystal clear and pure.

Ayanna gripped Marya's arm, tugging her to the taffrail. "Look."

Where the accursed Island had once stood, a lone object pierced the water. Shading her eyes with her hand, Marya recognized it as the Stone where countless villagers had died and the Prince had shed his innocent blood to redeem his people.

As she watched, the ship drifted nearer and the Stone grew—not merely expanding, but actually growing and changing shape as a young sapling matures into a tree strong enough to withstand the tempests. The Stone became an island, fair and green, covered with beautiful trees, hanging vines, and radiant flowers. Wreathed in sunshine and filled with the fragrance of a thousand flowers, the green island sang to the accompaniment of lilting birdsongs.

The Prince lowered his arms and faced the villagers. "The Island as it was meant to be."

"Please, sir." The boy stared wonderingly at the Prince. "Are we going back there now?"

The Prince ruffled his hair. "Soon, but first, we must go to the Kingdom."

The warm breeze sprang up again, filling the shimmering sails and sending the white ship flying across the water. Abandoning the wheel, the Prince strode to the bow of the ship, hefted the boy, and set him behind the dove figurehead.

His laughter drifted back across the deck. "I see it!"

Marya raced to the side of the ship and saw, directly before them, a long, low white shore. The shore of the Kingdom.

"Home," a soft voice whispered beside her. The dark-haired young woman Marya had seen on the shore of the accursed Island leaned across the rail with her arms outstretched as if it was the only thing keeping her from taking flight and soaring ahead of the ship. Her eyes shimmered with tears. "At long last, we are home."

Waiting on the edge of the water stood a figure crowned in glory—the King. As the white ship neared the crystal shore, he raised his hand in welcome, and Marya fell to her knees, bowing her head in reverence. As she raised her head, she saw the King's gaze meet that of the Prince; she beheld the look that passed between them.

In it were written many things—the tale of a father's incredible love, of suffering and victory, of a people ransomed, a promise kept, and darkness slain.

The Prince leapt from the ship as the keel scraped to a gentle stop on the sandy beach, and the Father and the Son embraced. Joy filled Marya's heart to overflowing. She could not keep silent. It burst forth in the only possible way, and so with the other villagers, she raised her voice in a song of praise and thanksgiving.

The King stood his Son at his right hand, and even the brilliant light of the sun dimmed before the incandescent radiance of their glory.

The Prince beckoned the villagers forward, laughter ringing in his voice and shining in his eyes. "Come," he invited. "My Father awaits you!"

~ *Not the End* ~

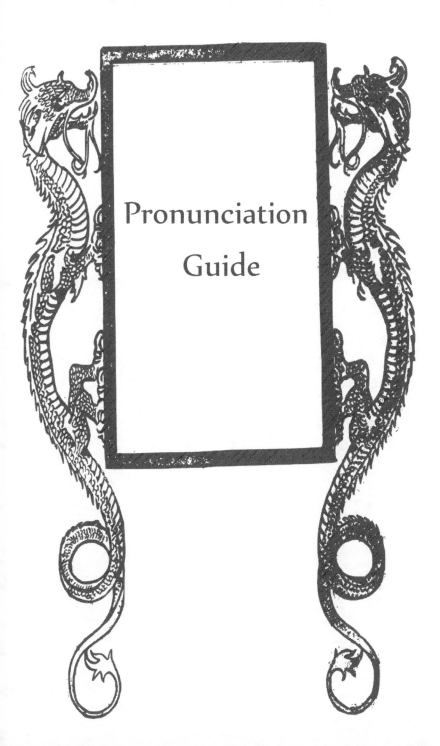

Pronunciation

Guide

Arientyl: AR-ee-n-till

Ayanna: AYE-an-nah

Bjorn: Bee-YORN

Corridan: CORR-i-DIN

Hadriel: Had-dree-ELL

Hoag: HOEG

Maddrel: Mad-DRELL

Marya: MAR-yah

Rahedhenaur: Rah-ETH-en-au-er

Roald: ROLLD

Taban: TAH-bahn

Acknowledgments

There is always a story behind any story...

Any book that moves from story spark to printed work goes through a long, and often tedious, process. But for *Out of Darkness Rising,* that process seemed even longer than most. What began as a short story penned in a fit of procrastination from a dreaded high school algebra course soon became a novella. Now, almost six years after it first appeared on paper, I'm so excited that you can finally hold it in your hands!

I owe a heartfelt thank you to:

• my sister, Brynne, who read an early draft of the short story and graciously pointed out all the rules that, at the time, I didn't even *know* I was breaking,

• my parents who backed me up each step of the way and encouraged me to trudge on and never give up hope,

• all of my courageous friends and long-suffering family who braved the blistering cold and put in many hours to film and edit the book trailer—y'all are the best!

A special thank you goes to:

• Scott Appleton for first believing in the unpolished work that was *Out of Darkness Rising*

• Nichole White for believing in it now

• Ann Bare for helping to hone the manuscript

• Darko Tomic for a cover that completely blew aside my wildest dreams.

And thank you, dear reader, for picking up this book.

Author Bio

Gillian Bronte Adams is a sword-wielding, horse-riding, coffee-loving speculative fiction author from the great state of Texas and the dreamer behind the Songkeeper Chronicles. During the day, she manages the equestrian program at a youth camp. But at night, she kicks off her boots and spurs, pulls out her trusty laptop, and transforms into a novelist.

To find out more about Gillian and her writing, please feel free to visit the following sites:

Website: gillianbronteadams.com
Facebook: https://www.facebook.com/gillianbronteadams
Twitter: https://twitter.com/theSongkeeper